JJ WEATHERILL
Grand Opening for Murder

First published by Weatherill Essentials - Publishing 2024

Copyright © 2024 by JJ Weatherill

All rights reserved. No part of this publication may be reproduced, stored or transmitted in any form or by any means, electronic, mechanical, photocopying, recording, scanning, or otherwise without written permission from the publisher. It is illegal to copy this book, post it to a website, or distribute it by any other means without permission.

This novel is entirely a work of fiction. The names, characters and incidents portrayed in it are the work of the author's imagination. Any resemblance to actual persons, living or dead, events or localities is entirely coincidental.

This ebook file is rights protected and can not be reproduced, copied or sold by any party other than the publisher or author.

First edition

ISBN: 9798883384485

*This book was professionally typeset on Reedsy.
Find out more at reedsy.com*

This book is dedicated to my real-life mother-in-law, Kristy. Much like Catherine in this book, she hated me in the beginning. Now I'd say we get along pretty well!

This book is dedicated to my friend Betty, who first introduced me to mystery (in school, where she wrote some of the best!) and fed my love for it by lending me so many books and recommending so many great authors.

This book is also dedicated to my third child, who introduced me to my own much younger best friend. Thank you, Via

Contents

Acknowledgments	iii
MAP AND KEY	iv
CHARACTERS	vi
Prologue	viii
1 Best Friend To The Rescue	1
2 Welcome to America	8
3 Grand Opening Eve	15
4 Opening Day	24
5 Adrenaline Crash	35
6 Grand Opening For Murder	40
7 Closed For Business	45
8 The Sleuth Returns	49
9 Take One For The Team	63
10 Fingerprints & Family Drama	72
11 Forensics & Dinner Dates	77
12 Miles Makes An Arrest	88
13 Suspects & More Suspects	104
14 Kiss and Make Up	113
15 Hiding in Trees	128
16 We Are Nowhere	137
17 Bellhops & Doctor's Notes	147
18 Dinner Parties & Murderous Girlfriends	158
19 Horses At The Inn	170
20 Fishing For Evidence	178

21 A Story To Tell	187
22 A New Beginning	194
About the Author	203

Acknowledgments

I want to thank my husband, DJ for all of his love and support. He's not a reader but he loves that I am and he encourages and helps me every step of the way.

I want to thank my ex-husband and my kids for their support in my writing for so long. I couldn't have started this career without them and I love them very much.

I want to thank my Australian family, Matthew, Kristy, Tycan, DJ, and Sebastian for all of the love, support, and kindness they showed to me when I showed up on their doorstep needing a place to stay. I will never be able to thank you enough.

I want to thank my friend Betty for giving me the love of Cozy Mystery that led to these books.

I want to thank my friend Kelly for all of the support she's given to me not only in writing but in my personal life too.

I want to thank my beta readers, author friends, irl friends, and my family for their unwavering support now and in the past.

MAP AND KEY

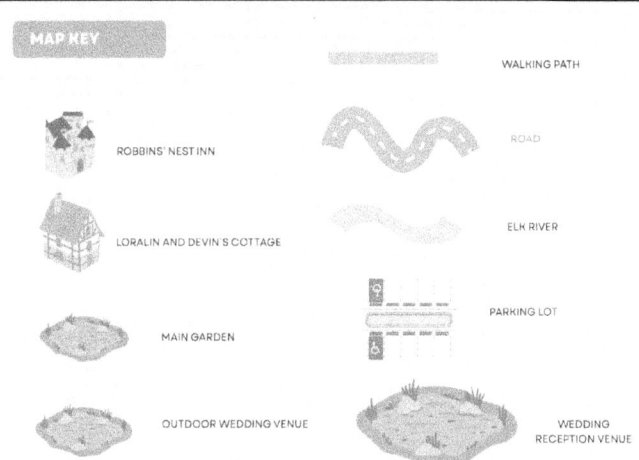

CHARACTERS

MAIN CAST

Loralin Robbins - *51 years old. Inherited the Inn from her grandparents and decided to renovate and reopen after years of being closed down. Best Friends with Devin Wentworth*

Devin Wentworth - *25 years old. Helped his parents run their hotel in Tasmania, Australia. Decides to move to America to escape his family and help Loralin run the Inn. Best Friend to Loralin Robbins.*

Miles Robbins - *51 Years old. Detective for the Elk River Police Department. Ex-husband of Loralin Robbins. He's a stereotypical short-statured, middle-aged 'local cop'.*

SUPPORTING PLAYERS

Catherine, Mark, and Trevor Wentworth - *45, 47, and 12 years old. Devin's family, who follow Devin to America to make sure he's safe with Loralin. Catherine hates Loralin and isn't afraid to let her know.*

Meredith Robbins - *50 years old. Freelance caterer. For her, cooking is life. Miles' new wife. Friends with her husband's ex.*

Heather Robbins - *25 years old. Labor and Delivery Nurse at Natrona County Medical Center. Loralin and Miles' oldest daughter. Devin's ex-girlfriend.*

Hanna Robbins Buchanan - *22 years old. Married to Matthew Buchanan. Lives in Evanston, WY. Loralin and Miles' youngest daughter. Works in IT.*

Chef Pierre Marqui - *In his 70s. Chef of the Inn's Restaurant. Known for his temper. There's something fake about him.*

Penny - *Early 40s. The Robbins' Nest Inn's head housekeeper. She's known Loralin her whole life. Close frenemies with Lisa Marie and Chloe.*

Lisa Marie and Chloe - *Early 40s. Housekeepers at the inn. Frenemies with head housekeeper Penny. Lisa Marie takes a liking to Devin.*

Don Peterson - *51 years old. Known as Handsy Don because he is known for being annoying in his pursuit of love. Chief of Police in Cheyenne, Wyoming.*

Prologue

Treacherous wintertime ice still popped up in select places along the eastern fork of the Elk River. The icy cold water wound through the town of the same name in central Wyoming. As Loralin Robbins made her way along the bank, she felt so at peace. This haven, tucked deep in the pines, was one of her favorite places on earth. This portion of the river ran right through the property she had inherited from her grandparents years ago. The dream she'd had since she was a child was about to come true. She could barely contain her excitement.

The cell phone in her pocket rang and vibrated, reminding her that she still had so much work to do. She should probably get back to her home office and do some of it. It would be a shame if the Grand Opening of the Robbins' Nest Inn snuck up on her before she was ready.

She would answer the call on the way back to the house she'd recently renovated for herself on the property. "Hello, this is Loralin."

A familiar voice rang out over the line, and her stomach felt like it was about to take flight out of her mouth. Sometimes she could sense when bad things were going to happen. And when her business partner George Conrad's garbled voice came out of the speaker, she had no clue what to expect other than bad news.

"George, can you repeat that? I can barely hear you."

The words she heard next sent her world spiraling. "I've married the widow Shriner, and we're going to tour Europe. You'll have to find a new partner!"

The line went dead, and Loralin sighed, looking toward the heavens. What next? Although she wasn't relying on George for money to start the business, thank goodness, he was going to help her run the place in exchange for a small salary and a place to live. And what was with him marrying the former Chairman of the board of Casper's hospital? How had they even met? Now she had no manager, no handyman, and no one to help her greet the guests for one shift a day. What the hell was she going to do now?

Loralin's new home greeted her like a favorite comfy blanket. It wrapped her in sweet memories. She loved the three-bedroom cottage just to the east of the inn and had spent many days here as a young girl when her grandparents called it home. The best part was that now it was hers, and although she'd modernized it just a bit, it was still cute and cozy like her grandmother would have wanted it to be.

When her stomach grumbled, she decided to put the new problem of finding a manager to the side and headed for her favorite room in the house. The kitchen was completely modernized, featuring the best appliances and stunning quartz countertops. The only thing that still reminded her of her grandmother in the room was the sunny garden-themed decorations she'd scattered around the space.

Just as she started pulling sandwich makings out of the refrigerator, her phone once again rang and buzzed from her pocket. This time caller ID told her it was her oldest daughter, Heather. "Hey, kiddo. What's up?"

"Hey, Mama! I heard through the hospital grapevine that

George might be skipping town. I'm sorry if he did that to you." That was Heather, the nurse for you. She didn't beat around the bush, even with her patients. Ever.

"I'm fine, dear. I just had a walk along the river," Loralin teased, rubbing it in that her daughter hadn't asked how she was. "And yes, this thing with George might be a terrible mess, but I'm going to fill my stomach before thinking about it too much."

"Since it's true, I have a solution," Heather stated, her voice rising almost to a singsong level.

Loralin turned her full attention to her daughter as she set the last of the sandwich makings on the counter. Heather always seemed to have a solution, but maybe that's because she was a nurse at the local hospital, a half hour away in Casper. She loved finding solutions for her patients. "Okay, I'm listening. What's on your mind?"

"Well, I have an idea about whom you could hire to take George's place." The minute she said those words, Loralin knew who she was talking about, and there was no way she could go there.

"No, absolutely not! I couldn't do that to you." Heather wanted her mutual friend zoned friend to be the one Loralin hired. But that was out of the question. When Loralin and the young man became friends, rumors had flown through town and all over the internet for a while until people just accepted it. Loralin Robbins was the fifty-one-year-old lady with the twenty—five-year-old best friend. "And after what his mother did to try to make it look like we… Just no. I can't hire Devin!"

The friendship had been a surprise to everyone involved. He'd messaged Loralin to seek her advice, and they'd never stopped messaging. How likely was it that two people, just over twenty years apart, would like the same music and movies and have the same views on religion and politics? The fact that the friendship between the two young adults was a long-distance thing, from America to Australia, and there wasn't much attraction, helped the friendship between Loralin and Devin keep going. It wasn't something anyone could explain, so she'd stopped trying. She learned to live with the accusations that she'd stolen her daughter's 'boyfriend'.

"It's okay, Mama. Devin and I have made peace, and his mother is… something I can't bring myself to say in front of my mom. Don't pass up this opportunity!" Now the daughter sounded more like the mother. "You know he's perfect for the job. He's been working at the family hotel in Tasmania since he was a little boy. He would be great, and you'd have him close. It's stupid that you guys can't see each other and must be so careful because his mother is right there all the time."

"Alright, I'll think about it. Now, tell me what's going on at the hospital. I hear you're about to get new owners." It was still quite uncomfortable discussing Devin with Heather. It was best for everyone if the subject was changed.

"So far so good," Heather said. "They keep insisting that there will be no major changes. I guess we'll see."

Heather was the type of person who never showed emotion on her face, but her voice always betrayed her. "You don't sound so confident about it."

"It's not that, Mama," she said with a sigh. "You know that awful, evil, Phyllis?"

"Oh, you mean Nurse Ratched as she's known behind her back?" Loralin knew the woman well; she had been a year behind her in school. She hadn't changed a bit in all those years.

"Yeah. She's up for head nurse in labor and delivery. If she gets it, I'm toast." She actually sounded scared.

"Because your father chose me over her. I'm so sorry, sweetie." There were just some things that a parent couldn't protect their child from.

"It's okay, Mom," she said, her voice sounding less and less burdened. "It's not your fault. We're all hoping the new owner will listen to our complaints."

"Me too… hey Heather, I have another call. Can I get back to you tomorrow? Devin's name and number flashed across the screen as she pulled it away from her face.

"Sure. Bye, Mama."

Loralin clicked over to the new call, and her best friend's desperate voice came over the line. "Loralin, help me!"

Oh boy. Normally, those words coming out of Devin's mouth would have worried Loralin, but right now, for some reason, she felt like she might just have hit the jackpot. "What's wrong?"

"My mother. I don't think I can take it anymore. I need to get out of here, but I only have three-quarters of the money saved up."

"Well then, my dear best friend, do I have a proposition for you?" It was finally time to get her best friend out of the mess he had been in for years. A move from Australia to America was just what he needed.

1

Best Friend To The Rescue

The grand opening of the Robbin's Nest Inn was only a few days away, and the more excited Loralin got, the harder it was for her to concentrate. But on this day, she knew exactly what she was doing. She was still excited, perhaps more excited than she'd ever been, but her focus was unbroken because today she would be seeing her best friend in person for the first time.

Devin had never let her help him out financially before, but when the cost of his plane ticket had become part of the hiring package she created for him, he'd finally agreed to come. Unfortunately, his parents had insisted on accompanying him so they could 'make sure he was 'safe'. Loralin was footing the bill for that, too. It was the only way to get her best friend slash manager slash handyman here without his mother trying every trick in the book to keep him there, including getting him arrested.

Luckily, the entire Wentworth family had passports and had secured travel Visas. Devin had been planning to move to the States and work for a while. Unfortunately, his mother had done everything in her power to make sure he never had quite enough money. There was always one expense or another. She'd raised his rent three times in six months to keep him with her. But now, because of the job Loralin offered, Devin could be free. At least once his parents ensured his safety and flew back home, he could be free. She tried not to dwell on that aspect of the deal too much. The thought of having his mother underfoot gave her a splitting headache.

This was one time that Loralin was grateful she lived in a place where the closest international airport was small and not usually very busy. She wouldn't have to fight crowds, and Devin and his family would have easy and quick access to their luggage.

At the noon hour, the tiny airport was nearly deserted, and Loralin was able to walk right in and find out where she would need to wait. Little did she know, being alone was probably not good for her nerves, because once she sat down to wait and there was no one else there but the nearby ticket agents, she started to tremble.

She knew everything about Devin, and he knew everything about her, so why should she be nervous? The only difference would be that she could reach out and touch him if she wanted, and she wouldn't have to depend on the internet connection to determine whether she could see him clearly.

Just as her nerves were about to get the best of her, she heard footsteps nearby, and when she looked up, her oldest daughter was standing in front of her. "Heather? What are you doing here?"

"I figured you could use the support. Seeing your best friend in person for the first time is a big deal." She sat down next to her mother and took her hand.

"Yeah, but I'm sure Devin and his mother are the last people you want to see." Loralin felt better, but her insides were still all shaky and fluttery.

"It's okay, Mama. You'll see how well Devin and I can get along if we have to." She squeezed her mother's hand.

"Alright. I won't argue. I like having you here for support."

The two women didn't talk as they sat holding hands. And then the arrival of flight 205 was announced. Loralin dropped Heather's hand and stood up, moving forward to await the arrival of the plane's occupants. She wasn't nervous anymore, just excited. She'd waited three years to hug this man, and now she couldn't wait to actually do it. What would it be like having late-night chats with her best friend, sitting in her living room, and not over a bad internet connection?

The door opened and out came a few passengers who had arrived on the same flight. For some reason, they looked irritated. And then the screeching voice of Catherine Wentworth came rushing out mere seconds before she appeared. The woman not only sounded more annoying in person, but she also looked more annoying, too. And when her eyes fell on Loralin, she felt like she was about to be murdered.

Loralin ignored the woman as her best friend came into sight. Her actions after that were automatic. The whole world seemed to disappear as she hurried over to him and took him into her arms. "God, it's so good to see you!"

Devin chuckled and finally hugged her back. He was an admitted non-hugger. "Wow, I could get used to this."

"See, I told ya they were hot for each other," Catherine snarled.

Heather stepped between the unpleasant woman and her mother and whispered. "Just ignore her, Mama."

"I agree," Devin said, reluctantly releasing Loralin. "Hello, Heather." The off-and-on friends smiled at each other, but that was it for their exchange. Maybe Heather had been telling the truth that they had come to terms with the friendship and all of the rumors and accusations of the last three years.

"Loralin, I'd like you to meet my mother, Catherine, my father, Mark, and my little brother, Trevor."

The first smile of greeting went to Devin's mother, but it was returned with a snarl, so Loralin moved on to his father, who graciously shook her hand. When she turned to Trevor, the little boy rushed to get a hug. She gladly returned it. The young man had been taught to hate her, but they'd come to a treaty somewhere along the line, and now he seemed to like her.

* * *

All the way back to the inn, Loralin and Devin talked like they had never lived 8900 miles apart, and Catherine pouted and seethed. Every time she hit the brakes, she almost wished the woman would go flying through the windshield. But instead of braking hard to keep her in check, she made sure she followed all rules and laws of driving so the woman wouldn't have one more thing to complain about.

"I sure hope the room is nice and not some rent-by-the-hour slum," Catherine huffed from the passenger seat.

Loralin's grip tightened on the steering wheel as she turned to glance at her best friend's mother. "All of our rooms are of the highest quality, I assure you. I'm sure you'll be satisfied with the accommodations. The first few nights, however, you will be staying at my house. The inn is not quite ready to be occupied."

"There better not be construction noise," she grumbled as she turned to look at her husband. A glance in the rearview mirror told Loralin that he and Devin were mortified at Catherine's actions.

"I'm sure renovations are over, dear," Mark said with a sigh. "I'm sure she just meant that they are dressing up the rooms and making sure everything works properly before letting people stay there."

"That's exactly what I meant." Loralin had just about had enough of the woman, but for the sake of Devin and his little brother, she would continue to play nice. She was so glad that Heather was not still with them because she would have let loose on the woman ages ago.

******

Loralin made sure everyone was settled into her guest rooms for a bit of sleep for the jet-lagged family. Catherine and Mark were in one of the two spare rooms, and Devin and his brother would share the second one. Right then, though, Devin was not willing to sleep. He was ready to check out the inn. She had no problem obliging him because she was excited to show her baby off to the person she was closest to in the world.

"Come on, Loralin! Let's go to the inn!" Devin grabbed her hand and pulled her out of the hallway. Both of them heard his mother's response to the platonic handhold.

"Old slut cunt is gonna corrupt my son."

Loralin turned to Devin. "It seems your mum is using that vile word in the American sense and not in the less triggering sense that Australians seem to use it."

Devin chuckled and nodded his head in agreement as they walked down the pathway that led to the inn, still holding hands and enjoying the comfort of it.

Loralin turned to the man beside her. "Can I ask you something?"

"Uh, yeah. Is something wrong?" The worried look on his face almost made her chuckle.

"Nothing's wrong. I'm just wondering how I would corrupt you? You're a grown man and have your own mind and…" I finished the sentence with a shrug.

Devin laughed and started moving again. "She thinks that since we met when I was seventeen and because of her crazy idea that we have more than a friendship, you prey on young boys."

She chuckled. "Well, I guess I did take you away from your family and country. But as we both know, that's all I've done. And you were well over eighteen when we started messaging."

"Hey," he said, pulling her to a stop again. "You didn't take me from anything. My mother did that. Her verbal abuse of you and our relationship made me want to leave. She made me need to leave to survive. All you did was extend the invitation."

She shrugged her shoulders and pulled him back down the path. "Look up." If it wasn't for her… Damn, she didn't know whether to blame herself or be glad she'd helped him.

When Devin raised his head, a big smile overtook his face. "Wow, she's a beaut! So much more amazing in person than in the pictures you sent."

"You really think so? You're not just saying that to make me feel good?" She wondered how she could be so insecure about this one thing. But then again, this was now her whole life, and it was time to make it or break it.

"I would never do that," he said seriously right before he pulled her in for another hug.

"Umm," she squeaked as he squeezed her hard. "I never thought I'd see the day that you would initiate a hug."

"Yeah, well…" He slowly pulled away from her and grabbed her hand again. "It must be the weird air here in America."

Loralin laughed the rest of the way up the long porch to the front door of the inn. "You do know that the air here is the same as the air in Australia, right?"

A slight blush colored Devin's face. "I know, but at the time it sounded good. I'm gonna blame America for anything weird that happens. You know that, right?"

With a playful sigh, Loralin pulled out her keys and opened the door of the inn. "Yeah, I know."

2

Welcome to America

Loralin was pretty sure Devin loved the inn even more once he'd had the VIP tour. After a couple of hours looking at the intricate woodwork that laced the moldings and staircases, lush, warm-colored carpets and rugs, and rooms with warm down-home decorations and quilts on every bed, the sun was setting. Devin was getting tired, even though he would never admit it. "Hey, let's go get your family up and have some dinner. Then you all can go back to bed and hopefully not be too jetlagged tomorrow."

*****

Reservations had already been made, so Loralin didn't have to worry about having her cooking insulted yet. But everything between the house and the restaurant in Boone, a town twenty miles away, was fair game. Elk River had a couple of good, down-home restaurants, but Boone had a bar and grill that she figured Devin and his family would like better.

Luckily for everyone, Catherine was starting to feel the jet lag and was quiet for most of the trip. It wasn't until they hit the outskirts of Boone that she decided to say something.

"There sure isn't much in this state, is there?" Her remark was quiet but still snide.

"Beautiful scenery," Loralin said softly. "You know, one of the major things your country is known for." She braced herself for a harsh retort from Catherine and admonished herself for inviting such a response. But it never came. The most she got from her was a small grunt. The permanently grouchy woman just turned and looked out the window for the last two miles to the restaurant. Did Loralin dare hope that the animosity was over?

It didn't take long for Catherine Wentworth to show her true colors again. Right after they sat down at a table, the waitress approached to welcome them and ask for a drink order. As soon as the young woman left, Catherine started to complain about the service. The weird thing for Loralin was that she was complaining not about bad service but that it was too attentive, too quick, and too good. Apparently, where they were from, service was minimal, and getting a waitress who loved her job and her customers was bad.

Loralin took out her phone and texted Devin. "Will anything ever be right for her?"

He quickly texted back. "No. Not unless she's asleep. And even then, it's questionable."

"Look at those two," Catherine snarled. "Can't even stop sending love notes at dinner."

Devin tightened up next to Loralin, and out of instinct, she reached over and put her hand on his arm. Pulling it back quickly, she realized her mistake a second too late. She'd given Catherine something else to complain about. Luckily, though, her husband came to the rescue.

"No, dear. I doubt it was a love note. They were probably

complaining about you and your bad attitude."

She had never seen Devin that shocked in the whole time she'd known him, but Loralin felt every bit of it as he froze beside her. The whole table froze, including Catherine. Everyone was braced for the storm that was sure to come.

"I think that's the first time Dad's ever made Mum speechless," Trevor finally squeaked out. It seemed America was making everyone in the Wentworth family brave. Following a few more moments of shocked silence, the waitress reappeared with the drinks, and at least for the moment, all was forgotten.

*****

Thanks to Devin and Trevor, who both ate like teenagers, the appetizers they ordered disappeared quickly, and the table grew quiet. Every word that Loralin thought to say, she decided against because she was afraid of the wrath of Catherine it would bring. Devin's mother didn't seem to have the same problem. "So, when are ya two gonna admit that the only reason ya invited my son here is to fu…"

"Catherine!" Mark said loud enough for the whole restaurant to hear. "Enough. They are both adults. If that's what they want to do, we have no say in it."

"But dad, that's not what we want to do. We are just friends. I don't know how many times I have to say it." Devin was angry but somehow defeated at the same time.

"I just meant that at this point it's none of our business and your mother needs to drop it," Mark said. If looks could kill, Catherine was in the middle of pulling the trigger on a gun right then and there.

Loralin wanted to curl up in a ball and die, but she knew she needed to speak up. "Catherine, I did not seduce your 17-year-old son. We talked a lot because he was seeking advice about

Heather, and then we grew close. That's it.

"It's not normal!" Catherine seethed. "A fifty-something woman and a twenty-something man is unnatural. They shouldn't even be friends."

"It's not like we could help it, mother," Devin snarled back at her. "It just happened, and you're going to have to learn to live with it."

It was pretty obvious that Mrs. Wentworth wasn't used to her son sticking up for himself. Whether it was the American air or a new confidence he found in his new life, no one knew. But Loralin loved it. She'd been after him to stick up for himself for years.

"It's time to leave them alone now, Catherine," Mark said. "They are friends, and we need to accept it. Hell, I was friends with your mother, and you never had a problem with that."

Catherine was quiet for a moment, and everyone could see the venom building inside her. "And ya woulda fucked her given half a chance. Hell, for all I know, ya did."

Mark Wentworth looked like he'd been slapped. "You know damn well I never would have done that because I love ya. Why the hell do you think I stood by you all these years!" His wife looked like she'd been knocked down a peg, but then rose again.

"But she's his girlfriend's mother. I saw the I love yous in their texts. That whore stole her own daughter's boyfriend."

"Enough!" Loralin demanded. "I did not steal my daughter's boyfriend. They were never a couple. And those I love yous you saw were because he needed a mother figure who cared, and I became that. He loved me like a second mother. And then we became friends, and now he loves me like a best friend."

"How dare you, ya bitch. I'm a good mother!" Catherine

somehow managed to keep her angry tone quiet enough that nobody except those at the table heard. "I should have killed you the minute I knew something was going on between yous two!"

Everyone saw the minute Devin broke. He slammed his napkin down on the table, scooted his chair back, and stormed out of the restaurant. Loralin wanted nothing more than to run after him, but she had to pay the bill. He barely acknowledged her the whole ride home, and she wasn't quite sure why.

*****

Loralin pulled into a parking spot and turned off the car. The Wentworth family quietly left the vehicle and scattered in all different directions. Devin headed down to the river, and Loralin had to decide if she should follow him. Best friends were supposed to help each other when they were down, so she chose to head in the direction he'd gone. "Hey Dev, you okay?"

He remained quiet, but in the dark, Loralin thought she saw him shrug his shoulder before his posture slumped again.

"Come on, talk to me." She felt him shutting down, and that was the last thing either of them needed.

"Not much to talk about." His voice was soft, and the rushing of the river was nearly explosive because of spring runoff, so Loralin moved closer to hear him better.

"Is it your mom? Me? I'm sorry, I'll try not to fight with her anymore." It was such a delicate situation with Devin and his mom. Sometimes she thought she just made things worse by being in his life. But she'd tried to give him up, and it just wasn't possible. He meant too much to her to lose him, now or ever.

Devin sighed and turned his head to the side to look at her.

"It's Mum. She's starting to get to me. Maybe I should give up and go home to accept my fate. I mean, she'll have to die someday, and this ridiculousness will end."

"Oh my God, Devin! Don't ever say that. You have a right to be happy. You have a huge opportunity here to live your own happy life. You will not give it up because your mom makes you feel guilty or makes your life difficult. They'll be gone in a few days, and you'll be able to think straight." Loralin's voice was higher-pitched than normal, and her desperation was starting to show in her body language. She was slightly mortified to realize that she was tugging on his shirt sleeve like a petulant child trying to get their mother to give them money for candy.

Loralin was sure that if it were light enough to see, he would have tears of frustration just at the surface. His voice confirmed that fact for her. "I know. I'm so close to freedom, but when she gets like this, it's hard to believe I can do it."

"Well, you can," Loralin said as she pulled him into a hug. "I won't let her pull you back, no matter what I have to do."

"Thank you," he whispered into her hair as they stood there, not wanting to move from the comforting embrace.

"Well, well, look at the lovers hiding out by the river!" Devin pulled away from Loralin the moment he heard his mother's voice. "You don't have to hide. We all know this filthy cunt is ruining your life."

"Shut up, mother! Don't use that word here!" Devin had to breathe deeply to continue. "I'm serious, that's enough of your hate."

"Ungrateful brat!" Catherine turned and headed back to the house.

Devin and Loralin stood quietly for a moment while their

breathing calmed. "Well, I guess that's that," he said.

"Yeah," Loralin agreed with a shiver. Early spring nights were still chilly, especially by the river. "Now let's go watch a movie before bed. Tomorrow is a big day, and I want these bad memories replaced by some good ones. We've never actually watched a movie together in person before."

"I can't wait!" Devin said with a smile as he grabbed her hand and pulled her away from the bank and toward her cozy cottage.

3

Grand Opening Eve

Penny Carlisle rushed into the Robbins' Nest Inn, praying she hadn't just ruined her chance to shine at her new job. Being the Head of Housekeeping at the new inn was a coup; one that had cost her the longtime friendship of her former boss. He had not been happy when she'd taken the position at his biggest new competitor. "Loralin! I'm so sorry I'm late. My car picked today to get a flat tire, and my cell phone fell out of my pocket and broke while I was changing the tire."

Loralin couldn't help but smile. Penny was nothing if she wasn't a mess. Her whole life was a series of mishaps and bad luck. But the one thing she had going for her was that she knew how to clean, and she knew how to train people to clean as well as she did. In her capable hands, the Robbins' Nest Inn would be the cleanest hotel in the state. "It's okay, kiddo. Chloe and Lisa Marie have been holding down the fort by loading the cleaning carts. I know you had a plan, so go for it. The inn is in your capable hands now."

"Thank you, Loralin," Penny said. Her voice conveyed a sense of relief. "I won't be late again." She had just headed off when she was called back.

"Hey Penny, I wanted to introduce you to the Hotel Manager. Penny, this is Devin. Devin meet Penny. He'll be your immediate supervisor."

"Well, well, so we finally get to meet the young stud that took Elk River by storm." My slightly shy companion blushed at our head housekeeper's words."

"Umm. Uh. Well, it's nice to meet you, Penny. I look forward to working with you." It wasn't often one got to see Devin Wentworth blush and stammer at the same time. Loralin loved every minute of it.

"Same here, boss," Penny said with her characteristic smile.

Once the young woman was gone, Devin turned to look at Loralin. "So, everybody really does know about me here, huh?"

Loralin couldn't help but chuckle. "I was not exaggerating. Nowadays, however, people rarely, if ever, mention it anymore."

"Except for our head housekeeper," Devin grumbled as he left her side to go back to work.

For a brief moment, Loralin wondered if Penny, Chloe, and Lisa Marie had been the right choices for working in her hotel. At one point, they had been steady friends with a penchant for gossiping. Hopefully, the fact that the friendship had faded would keep them from getting into her business too much. She'd been through the wringer over Devin and didn't want to repeat the nasty gossip at the hands of her staff.

*****

For the third time within an hour and a half, Loralin signed an invoice handed to her by a truck driver. She was sure there were more last-minute supplies than there were ones she'd gradually stocked the hotel with. Now, there would be a fully stocked kitchen, lobby, and cleaning supplies closet. Things seemed to be coming together, but every once in a while, she had to stop and take a deep breath to refocus. There was still so much to do before the first guests checked in at eleven a.m. the next day.

"Loralin! Loralin!" Devin's voice bordered on panic. He'd been in the lobby, and she was at the delivery entrance. He was yelling, and that was something Devin Wentworth rarely did. Without a moment's hesitation, she headed for where she'd last seen him.

"What on earth is wrong, Devin?"

"The computers aren't working. They just died." She wasn't sure if he was angry, amused, or about to cry. Maybe he was all three. "Look at this, blank screens. I know computer basics, but I don't know anything about reservation systems. I can't even message the customers with their reminders because I don't have their numbers."

"Really!" Loralin hated bad stress, and this was the ultimate stressor in an inn. "What the hell else is going to happen today!"

"I guess we should call your IT guy," he said. "I mean, we do have an IT guy, right?"

Loralin blushed and leaned against the counter, where she let her head fall with a thump. "We *had* an IT guy. He's now on a cruise with his new, rich wife. George was not only supposed to be my manager and caretaker, but he was a computer science teacher in another life and had learned this system specifically for this job."

"Call another one?" Devin suggested with a shrug. "I mean, computer guys are everywhere, right?"

Loralin stood upright and laughed. "Maybe in the city. But

here in Elk River, we don't have anything like that. Hell, I wouldn't even know who to call in Casper, even."

Devin looked like she'd slapped him. "Then what the hell do we do now? I'm out of my element here. At home, we do all reservations on paper."

"Hey, Mama," a sweet voice interrupted them. Loralin's frown morphed into a smile. Her youngest daughter, who had moved across the state to Evanston, was now standing in the lobby, bringing cheer to the whole room.

"Oh, Hanna, you are a sight for sore eyes." Loralin hurried to her daughter and caught her in an embrace. "Why are you here? Shouldn't you be at home?"

"Oh, Mama," she said with one last squeeze of her mother's shoulders. "I would never miss your grand opening. You know that."

"So," Devin cut in with a sly smile. "This is the famous computer guru Hanna Robbins?"

"The one and only," Hanna chimed in with a flourish.

"Hanna, baby, this is Devin. Devin, this is Hanna."

"Wow," the young woman said in disbelief. "I never thought I'd get to meet you. Sometimes I just thought you were a figment of Mom and Heather's imaginations."

"What, I'm not?" Devin said with a cheeky smile that quickly turned serious. "What do you know about hotel reservation computers?"

"Uh, well, I know a decent amount. I worked in reservations at a hotel in Laramie during college. And of course, I made sure to learn everything about the hotel's computers. It's just kinda my thing.

"Thank God!" Devin said, grabbing her hand and dragging her around the front desk. "Can you help? Please. Fix this hunk of junk."

Hanna laughed and immediately started hitting the keys. "Computers are never hunks of junk. They are just... well, they are similar to temperamental toddlers. You just have to know how to finesse them. There, all fixed. And it won't happen again."

"Am I just stupid?" Devin asked. "What was wrong with it?"

Loralin put her arm around her daughter and squeezed. "She's a miracle worker."

"No, Mama," Hanna said, blushing. Praise from her mother was always extra special. "There is a shortcut to turn off the system, and I just disabled it. Somehow, someone must have accidentally hit it."

Devin grinned. "It's okay, Hanna, you can say it. Your mother's useless best friend is the one who hit the keys."

Loralin noticed Hanna looking at her and quirked an eyebrow, telling her daughter that she would explain Devin's comment at a later time. "Well, Mama, Devin, I'm going to head over to my hubby's parents' house. We're staying there so we don't get in the way here. Heather says you have a full house right now."

"Give me another hug," Loralin said. "And you and Matthew are coming to our celebratory dinner tonight."

"Thanks, Mama. We'll be there." A kiss on the cheek was followed by the young woman turning and heading for the door.

Once she was gone, Loralin turned to her pouting Manager. "Devin Marshall Wentworth, I don't ever want to hear you say that again. Especially if there are customers nearby."

The young man looked momentarily stumped, and then it dawned on him. "I'm sorry, Loralin. I mean, Boss Lady. It's a habit. I'll keep it in check."

When he turned away, it broke her heart. His self-esteem sure had taken a beating throughout his life. "Dev, you are not now and never have been useless, you hear me? I don't care how many times your mother, your classmates, or anyone else said you were; you are the most amazing person I've ever met, and I need you to remember that."

"Thanks, Loralin," he said quietly. She knew he didn't believe her, but someday, if she had anything to say about it, every bad name people had called him would cease to exist in his vocabulary.

*****

The sun was getting low in the sky when Loralin and Devin locked up the inn and turned to give it one last look before heading home. In the morning, it was showtime. Loralin was more than ready for her moment in the spotlight. At least this time, the spotlight was a good thing, bright and also shining on many of the people she loved.

"So, do you feel like cooking a feast for everyone, or should we save the celebration for another day?" Devin was dead tired. She could tell. Running the little hotel his family owned was a piece of cake compared to the Inn. She knew he'd get used to it quickly enough, though.

"I never planned on cooking anything," she said with a smile. "My ex-husband's wife, the caterer, is providing dinner for us. I just hope your mother hasn't killed her or something by the time we get there."

Devin laughed. "Don't be surprised if you no longer get along with your ex's new wife. My mother ruins everything she touches."

Loralin grabbed her friend's arm, and they meandered

together down the path that led to her house. "I'm so excited, but I think I'll easily be able to sleep tonight," she admitted. "Thank goodness. I need to be on top of my game tomorrow."

"Same," Devin said, smiling and kissing the top of her head. "Shit, I'm sorry. Does that bother you?"

"No, Devin. You know that. If it's any consolation, Miles never once kissed me on top of my head. As far as I'm concerned, it's a friend thing."

"Good." Devin sighed. "You know I would never come on to you, right? Please don't start believing what my mother says."

They walked in silence for a while longer. Loralin was concerned for Devin. His mother was really getting to him. She needed to try to get his family out of there as fast as she could. "I never believe a word your mother says."

Devin's laugh was the last thing she heard before she walked into chaos. Catherine was yelling at the caterer, Meredith, but her ex's wife was giving as good as she got.

A loud whistle broke through the ruckus, and everyone went silent. Devin had to have been the loudest whistler she'd ever heard. He'd learned one summer working on a dairy farm with his uncle. The loudest whistle hopefully got the cow's attention the best. "Enough, mother! Let the woman do her job. Go take a walk by the river."

"Well, I never!"

"Come on, Catherine," Mark said. "Let's go." The couple walked out of the house, and everyone breathed a sigh of relief.

"Now I can get back to work," Meredith said as she headed back to the kitchen. "Dinner will be served in ten minutes." So many kitchen items had been delayed in arriving that Loralin hadn't asked the hotel's chef to cook. He would be there late into the night, after dinner, so he could get his kitchen organized. Meredith had come through in a pinch. And she was an amazing cook.

Loralin and Devin made their way into the living room, where Head Chef Pierre Marqui, Head Waiter Jason Parker, and Penny sat talking. Hanna, her husband, and Heather sat nearby. "Is everybody having fun?" Loralin asked. "Dinner will be served soon."

"Quite the entertainment you had scheduled," Pierre said with a huff. Loralin knew the older man was no more French than she was, but for years, everyone had played along. Bottom line was that his food was amazing, so it didn't matter if he wanted to use a fake French accent.

"Sorry about that," Devin said, diverting his gaze. "My mother is the Imperial Majesty of the drama queens."

"We'd probably get along perfectly," Penny said with a mischievous grin. "I was always the queen of drama in high school."

"Still are as far as I'm concerned," Jason said with a look and a grin at his best friend's sister. "I grew up with her, and man, she could cause some drama."

"That she could," Loralin said. "I think it's been about ten minutes. Should we head to the table?"

The group of family and management switched rooms, where at the large dining table, places were set for each guest. Loralin wondered if Meredith had spit in Catherine's food, but changed her thoughts when laughter threatened to bubble up. This dinner celebration was most likely going to be one that no one would ever forget.

*****

Loralin knew better than to let herself relax and enjoy the lively conversation and companionship that characterized the first part of the evening. But before she knew it, that is exactly what happened. That's why, when all hell broke loose, she felt like death was imminent.

Dessert, a tray of decadent crème puffs, ended up on the floor when Catherine told Meredith that she didn't know how to make a proper crème. That was Loralin's breaking point. She couldn't hold her tongue anymore, even for Devin. "That is it! You will not act that way in my house or my Inn. If you continue to be like that, you can fly yourselves right back to Australia!"

As Loralin stomped out of the dining room and Catherine was dragged away by the arms, they heard Chef Pierre entertaining the troops. "When I wasn't asked to cater this thing, I was offended. Now, I'm quite relieved. If that nasty woman had destroyed *my* dessert, it would have been the end of her!"

At that point, no one knew what the morning, the Grand Opening of the Robbins' Nest Inn, would bring, but Loralin hoped for a little less drama.

4

Opening Day

Loralin startled awake, realizing that she wasn't alone in her bed. But who was there? And then the memory of the night before came rushing back. Devin had been so upset by his mother's behavior that he'd come to her asking to talk, which they'd done until they both fell asleep.

Opening her eyes, her sight focused on a vision of Devin, fully clothed, holding her, her head resting on his chest. She hadn't had someone to snuggle with since her marriage ended, so it was kind of nice. Friendship was definitely much less complicated than relationships, but certain benefits could be shared by both.

"Good morning. You ready for today?" Devin asked before his eyes even opened.

"I am more than ready. We should probably get up before your mum…"

"Ya bloody whore! You just can't keep your grubby hands off my boy, can ya!" Catherine was fuming, her face red and her breathing accelerated. "You should be throttled for this!"

"Stop it, Mum." Devin sounded strong again, not defeated

like the night before. "We stayed up late talking and fell asleep. That's it." Without another word, he got up and left the room, brushing past his mother. Thankfully, she followed him, and Loralin was able to get up and get ready for the day in peace. If Catherine Wentworth ruined her big day, there was going to be hell to pay.

*****

"You ready, my friend?" Devin asked as he and Loralin approached the inn.

"More than. But I'm also nervous as Hell." Loralin had to do a last-minute inspection and brief the staff before accepting the first guests. She prayed every chance she got that things would go smoothly. If something was off that morning, her whole day would be off, and she wanted to enjoy her success rather than worry about it.

"I'm nervous too. I want this to work so badly for you. I've been with you the whole way, and I'm so glad I get to be a part of it." Loralin loved the genuine look of happiness on his face. It was about time Devin Wentworth could be happy. She'd waited years for this moment.

"Well then, let's do…" Devin's comment was interrupted by the ring of Loralin's phone.

"Oh, God. Why is the phone ringing? It only brings bad news! This is Loralin."

"Hey, boss, this is Penny. I'm so sorry, but the tire shop had to order the tires from Gillette. It will be another couple of hours before I can get there."

"Oh, Penny, I need you here this morning."

"I know, Loralin," she said apologetically. "I'm so sorry, but the girls know what to do, and I'll be there as soon as possible. I'll even stay late to make up the time if I have to."

Loralin sighed to herself. "Okay, Penny. I'll see you in a couple of hours." She hung up the phone and met Devin's questioning gaze. "It looks like I'll be a housekeeper for a few hours today."

Devin nodded and took the keys from his boss. Once the door was unlocked, she was ushered inside. "I'll help where I can. But first, you might want to put on one of the housekeeper shirts, so you don't ruin your new blouse. We have extras in the back."

*****

Loralin was seriously impressed with what Penny had done in just the one partial day she'd worked with Chloe, Lisa Marie, and the rest of the cleaning crew. The hotel was already almost spotless, and Loralin was able to leave them after an hour and get busy with her own tasks. "What's up?" came from her office doorway.

"Not much," she said, looking up at a smiling Devin. "What's up with you?"

"I'm done with what I needed to do. We open the doors in about twenty minutes, so you might want to get changed." Devin had walked in and sat in the chair across the desk from her.

"I think I like the idea of the t-shirt with the hotel name on it more than a fancy blouse. Once I finish up this report, I'll go check on the champagne and hors d'oeuvres for the opening reception, and then it will be go time."

"Sounds good," Devin said, standing up to leave. "By the way, I told my mum that if she pulls any shit today, I would put her ass on a plane back to Australia tonight."

"I hope it's enough to make her behave." Loralin put her hand on his cheek and smiled.

"It is. She won't want to leave me one second before she has to."

Loralin hoped he was right. If Catherine Wentworth ruined her big day… She couldn't even fathom it. She loved her best friend dearly, but that would hurt everyone involved, and she wasn't ready to lose him just yet.

*****

The Bellhop, Tony, was standing at his station, Devin was behind the desk with his Robbins' Nest Inn blazer on, and Loralin was standing at the front doors looking at her watch. The minute it clicked over to eleven a.m., she opened the big double doors to a waiting and excited crowd. Along with the guests, most of the town would be there to help her celebrate her accomplishment. The sea of familiar and unfamiliar faces swallowed her as the lobby filled up. Her heart swelled with pride the moment she saw Tony grab the bags of an older couple and put them in the cart to head upstairs. Their first guests had arrived.

Walking over to the front desk, Loralin stood next to Devin. "Good morning, Mr. and Mrs. Graves. It's good to have you back in Elk River if only for a short time." The older couple had once lived in a big house on the hill at the edge of town. They'd moved once retirement hit and only came back once or twice a year.

"Thank you, dear," Mrs. Graves said with a smile. "It's good to see you, too. How are Hanna and Heather?"

"They're doing great," Loralin said with a smile. Everyone's gazes had diverted to Mr. Graves, however. He and Penny were staring at each other like they'd seen a ghost. "Mr. Graves, is something wrong?"

"What? Oh no. Of course not. That young lady looks much

like you, Loralin. I thought maybe I was seeing double."

"Oh, Augustus, you are such a card," Mrs. Graves said with a laugh. The look in her eyes didn't match her tone of voice. "Let's get up to our room and freshen up, then come back for some champagne."

"Yes, let's," Augustus said, taking his wife's arm and leading her to the elevator.

Loralin couldn't help but wonder what that whole thing was about. It made her feel a bit out of sorts. And she couldn't believe they already had their first guest checked in. She thought for sure they would arrive later in the day. She also wondered why they weren't staying with their son, who lived only a few blocks away.

As more people approached the desk, Loralin took one of the reservation computers for herself and started checking people in alongside Devin and one other desk clerk.

"Yoo hoo, Loralin. Darling!"

"Wanda, it's nice to see you. Here for your annual visit to see your sister Thelma?"

"Yes, yes, dearie. I believe I have a reservation." The old woman fished around in her purse as if looking for something.

"I'm so glad to have your business, but why aren't you staying with your sister this year?" The two old sisters, both widows, were inseparable when they were together. Something was definitely off with the woman who used to babysit Loralin's girls when they were little.

"My sister has turned into a raging slut, and I refuse to stay with her and that cad Henry!" Loralin swore the old woman said Harumph at the end of her sentence.

"That's right," Loralin said, looking at the disdain in the older woman's eyes. "I'd heard that Thelma and Henry Watkins are seeing each other. Do they live together?"

"Well, no," Wanda admitted. "But…" She leaned in and lowered her voice to a whisper. "They do spend some nights together like a couple of young kids. It's shameful for a woman her age."

Loralin heard Devin choke down a chuckle. And the couple next to them gave Wanda sideways glances. It was amusing that she'd loudly announced that her sister, well-known in the community, was a slut, but she whispered the details of the situation.

"Well, welcome to the Robbins' Nest. I hope you'll bring Thelma and Henry in to see us at the restaurant." The woman nodded, took her key card, and headed to the elevator.

Loralin decided she would take one more reservation, and by then, Devin and the other clerk should be able to handle it. They were almost full, finally. She wanted to get out there and socialize. Most of the people there would expect it.

"Hi, there! Welcome to the Robbins' Nest. Can I get your last name?"

"Yes. Walden, Thomas, and Georgina." The man was stern-looking and held on tight to his son's hand as he checked them in.

"Okay, I've got you right here. You're in room 243. You turn right out of the elevator, and it's three doors down on your left."

The man nodded, and his wife quietly said, "Thank you."

"Would you like information on kids' activities in the area?" The poor boy looked bored.

"No, thank you, ma'am. My son will be doing activities with us." He nearly snatched the paperwork and key card out of her hand and herded his family to the elevators.

"Strange people," Devin said from Loralin's side. "They act like they are being followed or something; always looking over their shoulders. That poor kid probably won't be let out of their sight this whole vacation."

"I know. The way they were acting is quite disturbing." It added to the sense of unease that she'd had since the Graves checked in. "I'm glad they are only here for three days." Loralin made a mental note to keep an eye on the family. If the kid was in any danger, she would report it.

*****

"Hey, guys! Have you toured the hotel with one of the Bellhops yet?" A small group of women milled around by the windows that looked out over the mountains. They had all grown up with Loralin, and she considered them her closest local companions. Although today, she could take them or leave them. Devin was the subject of their whispers, and she wanted no part of it.

"Yes. Loralin, this place is amazing. You have done a wonderful job!" A woman wearing scrubs said from her perch on the arm of a plush chair.

"Thank you, Marybeth." Loralin had grown up next door to the nurse who worked at their local medical center. She was somehow always honest and kind to everyone she met.

"Yes," came from another woman standing and looking out the floor-to-ceiling windows. "It's quite quaint and cozy. I thought maybe you'd go away from the theme of every place in this damn town. Something more upper class."

"Well, Rhonda, quaint and cozy is why people visit Elk River, Wyoming. If they want an 'upper class' establishment, they can go to California or New York." Loralin sometimes felt sorry for her old friend. She'd had dreams of fame and the big city, only to marry a rich tycoon who fell in love with her small, boring hometown and moved her back there. She wasn't really a snob; she just wanted to turn everything into her vision of happiness.

Bidding her friends farewell, Loralin moved on to talk with other old friends, former teachers, former neighbors, and just about everyone who would be there to wish her well. "Hey, guys, what's going on?" she asked two of her waiters, Joseph and Steven, as they stood, heads together in the middle of the room.

"Sorry, Miss Loralin," Joseph said, his face turning red. "Everyone is talking about how Penny's ex-Sugar Daddy is here. Mr. Graves and his wife checked in as the first guests."

Loralin had to remain professional, but she wanted to let her mouth drop open in shock. Why had she never heard about this? And was Mrs. Graves oblivious too? She hadn't batted an eye when her husband had his episode of staring at the housekeeper, but she had seemed a little irritated. "Alright, boys, gossip time is over. Get back to work."

"Yes, ma'am," the two chorused before heading to opposite sides of the room to deliver champagne to guests.

The only ones Loralin hadn't talked to yet were Devin's family. She wanted to turn and run the other way, but she would do her job and be polite. This was business and not personal. "Hey, are you all having fun?" she asked.

"Yes!" Trevor said excitedly. "Everybody here loves you, Loralin."

She smiled back at the young boy and then looked up to see what his parents were thinking. "And you two?"

"Fine reception," Mark said with a warm smile. "And this place you've got here... It's a winner. You've done an amazing job."

"Thank you," Loralin said. She was a bit shocked to hear him say that. He usually tried to follow along with his wife. But she'd noticed he'd become much braver recently.

"Catherine, are you enjoying yourself?"

The woman huffed. "Well, the champagne is good, and the food is passable. Ya seem to have a lot of supporters."

Loralin wasn't sure if any of that was a compliment, but she was sure glad the words were somewhat positive and that her best friend's mother was behaving herself. "I'm glad you're doing well. I'll talk to you all later. I'm going to go check on my employees."

In the kitchen, Pierre was doing his best impersonation of Gordon Ramsey and the staff was loving it. They all knew the old chef was just a softie on the inside. As soon as she was satisfied that things were running smoothly, Loralin headed to the dining room, where the first of her guests and some locals were enjoying a brunch buffet. The happy chatter coming from all corners of the room was her answer to whether people were enjoying themselves.

Satisfied that the food service part of the inn was running properly, Loralin went in search of Penny and her crew. Hey, ladies, how are things going?" she asked, coming up on them stocking the hotel bathrobes that had just come in that morning.

"Opening day is so boring for us at first," Penny said, hiding a yawn. "Nobody has made a mess yet."

"Have those been delivered to the rooms?" Loralin had only been slightly upset that they were delayed.

"Yes, ma'am," Lisa Marie said with her cute impish smile. "Everything is good here."

Satisfied that nothing major was going wrong, Loralin headed to the front desk to check on Devin and his crew. All of the current guests were checked in, but that didn't mean the work was over. When she arrived back in the lobby, the desk clerk was handling questions and guest relations, but Devin was gone.

"He's in the office with his mother," Tony said as he polished the luggage carts. "I'd be careful going in there. They are both as angry as a swarm of hornets."

Loralin's heart skipped a couple of beats. It had been a great day, so why couldn't it last a bit longer? Catherine was determined to ruin everything. With a few deep breaths outside the office, she prayed that whatever was going on would stay in her office.

"Hey," Loralin said brightly as she opened the door. Catherine and Devin both looked up at her. "Is, umm, is everything okay?"

"I've had enough of walking around and seeing what my boy is in for. I want him to drop this stupid pipe dream and come home now!"

"Mum, I love it here. I love my job. I love Loralin, and I love this Inn. I'm not going anywhere." For once, his voice was steady when arguing with his mother. He was determined to stay, and he wasn't about to let anyone get to him. Or at least she hoped. That woman had a way of wearing people down.

"That's it, right? You want to be here alone with this cunt." Loralin rolled her eyes at the woman when she pointed to her. "You'll marry her, be childless, and be a widower before you're 40. You're wasting ya life, boy!"

"Whoa, wait a damn minute." Loralin wasn't the first to react to what Catherine had said, but she was the loudest. "First, I don't plan on dying that soon, and second, there is nothing romantic going on between us. You need to get that through your thick skull! I am not marrying Devin or anyone.

"Yer a lyin' cunt!" she yelled as she headed for the door. It wasn't until she hit the lobby that she finished her tantrum. "Ya stole your daughter's boyfriend. And you will steal him from this family over my dead body!" The stomping up the stairs to the room the Wentworth family would now occupy echoed through the downstairs.

Loralin didn't have to look up from the floor to know that the remainder of her guests had heard every word. Luckily, there weren't too many people left milling around. When she finally did look up, everyone was back to their own business. Her friendship with Devin had been big news, and people were curious now that he was finally there, but the scandal about it all seemed to be over. She would be forever grateful for that.

5

Adrenaline Crash

Loralin had to admit that the adrenaline of opening day was wearing off at a rapid pace. A fog seemed to envelop her the longer she was on her feet. By seven p.m., she was exhausted. Unfortunately, she had plans to stay at the inn for several more hours. Once she deemed everything was running smoothly, she would have a schedule with more reasonable shifts for herself and Devin.

Now it was time for the first dinner in the dining room, a test of sorts for the staff. Devin and his family, along with Hanna, her husband, and Heather, would be joining her. "Good evening, everyone." The first thing she noticed when she sat down was that Catherine was not there. There wasn't even a place set for her.

"Mother decided it would be best not to join us this evening," Devin whispered in her ear. "She is still furious at you and me."

"I'm sorry," she whispered back.

"Not something you should apologize for," he said with a genuine smile. "I just want to have some fun after such a long day."

Loralin felt the same way, so she put Catherine out of her mind and concentrated on ordering wine for the table. This was a celebration after all. "So, has everyone had a good day?" she asked as Steven brought their wine and started pouring glasses for everyone.

"Oh, Mama, I'm so proud of you," Hanna said, reaching over to grab her mother's hand. "This place is amazing, and word in town is that everyone loves it and is so happy for you."

Loralin hated compliments, but this one she would take graciously because it was the one compliment that meant the world to her. "Thank you, Hanna. Thank you, everyone. I must say this has been one of the best days of my life."

"Let's have a toast to Loralin," Devin proposed. "To my best friend, my boss, and the woman I am so happy to have in my life. Congratulations on a successful Grand Opening. And here is to much more success in the future!"

"Here, here!" rang out in a chorus around the table as glasses rose into the air.

Once the table was quiet again, Loralin lifted her glass. "I'd like to make a toast to the young man who came here at a moment's notice to help me out. He's the best friend a girl could have and an amazing manager for my lifelong dream. Thank you, Devin, so much for being here."

"My pleasure," he murmured with a smile as everyone toasted him.

"Can we just eat now? I'm starving." Trevor had had enough of the adult stuff. He wanted to dig into the food that would soon be arriving at the table. Laughter filled their quaint little corner of the dining room, and everyone agreed with the young boy. The toasts were nice, but the food by Chef Pierre was even better.

"I don't taste much French influence in the food," Devin said as he took another big bite.

"That's because Chef Pierre was born and raised in Wheatland, Wyoming. His real name is Peter Marks." Heather was the one to break it to him. His look of shock was soon replaced by the realization that he'd suspected it all along.

"I knew there was something off about him. He's a bloody fake."

"Oh, his name and accent might be fake," Hanna's husband Matthew said with a laugh. "But there is nothing fake about his talent as a chef. His food is amazing and always has been."

"I'm sorry," Devin said. "I didn't mean anything by it. His food is delicious, from the sandwiches we had for lunch to this steak. It's just a little shocking to find out."

"That's Elk River for you," Loralin teased. "If you want to find an oddball, just come to town and wait."

Devin couldn't help but laugh. "I didn't even have to come to town. I found one or two online."

Heather laughed at the reference to her, and Loralin looked momentarily offended but then relaxed into a small laugh. "Yeah, I guess you're correct there. I have been known to do my own thing on occasion. I'm for sure not one of the 'normal' people in town."

Dinner conversation wound down as people settled in to enjoy the rest of their meals. When the last plate was cleared from the table, Loralin stood, and her voice rang out through the dining room. "Can I have everyone's attention, please?" The room went instantly quiet.

"I just wanted to take this opportunity to thank everyone for being here and for making our grand opening such a big success. To our guests, friends, family, and everyone else who made this day possible. I love you all and appreciate your patience and kindness." There was a round of applause as she sat down, and Steven began passing out desserts.

"So, does anyone have any plans tonight?" Heather asked. "I'm just going to head home and go to bed. My shift tomorrow starts early."

"Devin and I are going to watch a movie," her mother chimed in. "After I go to town to get a few things I need, including popcorn."

Everyone was no longer looking at her but behind her. When she turned, Catherine Wentworth stood there. "Of course you are," she said under her breath. "Mark, Trevor, if you're done, I'd like for us to take a family walk through the woods before it gets too dark." Not once did she glance at the member of her family who was sitting next to Loralin.

Once the Wentworths left, things wound down quickly. Heather had a drive ahead of her, and Matthew and Hanna had plans with his cousins. Loralin was feeling slightly reenergized, but she didn't want to get up and go back to work. She still had a few administrative things to do while Devin made sure things were settled in for the night crew. "I'll meet you at the house when I'm done, Dev."

"Sounds good. I'll get there as soon as I can. I have to go see why Lisa Marie and Chloe were seen fighting outside the men's bathroom earlier. All I know is that it had something to do with who Penny had assigned to clean what. We might have to start writing down their tasks for them if they keep this up."

"Good luck," Loralin said, finally standing up from the table. "I'll see you later." With a quick kiss on his cheek, she walked in the opposite direction and settled into her office for some dreaded but necessary paperwork. This glorious but tiring day was almost over.

6

Grand Opening For Murder

This time, when Loralin and Devin woke up together, they weren't in her bed. They were on the couch in front of the television. Half a large bowl of popcorn sat on the coffee table. "I can't believe we fell asleep twenty minutes into the movie," she said with a groan. "I am so sore this morning. Getting older sucks."

Devin sat forward and ran his hands through his thick, dark hair. "I can believe it. We started it a couple of hours later than planned. And I was so exhausted. If getting older is what made you sore, why am I also sore?"

"You hang out with old people," Loralin teased. "I'm surprised your mother hasn't tried to use that to get us apart, too."

"Don't even think about it. She just might do that next. Go shower. I'll meet you in the kitchen."

Loralin took her time in her shower. The water was turned as hot as she could stand it, and she never wanted to leave. But she needed to get clean and get to work by seven a.m. She had less than an hour.

Despite the time crunch, instead of quickly applying soap, she took her time and kneaded her sore muscles, and washed her long auburn hair twice. Finally, once the peach-scented soap washed down the drain, she felt her stress go with it. Now she could enjoy her second day at the inn. It was all still so new and exciting, but also a bit nerve-wracking. Thank goodness she had Devin.

"You about ready?" Devin asked as she walked into the kitchen. "I think I'm going to grab something from the dining room for breakfast."

"I'm going to be a while. There are a few things I need to do before I head out," she said as she picked up her phone to make a call. "I'll meet you there?"

"Yeah," he whispered and headed out the door. He was pretty sure that his boss was checking up on her daughter since she'd had to drive thirty miles home in heavy Wyoming wind the night before.

*****

When Loralin arrived at the Inn, Devin was behind the counter, and Tony was trying to calm Chef Pierre. He was screaming about a knife. "What on Earth is going on here?" Loralin asked as she moved in between the bellhop and the chef.

"My favorite knife is missing!" he raged. "I come to work, and the knife that I got from Wolfgang Puck when I worked for him is gone." The anger was replaced briefly by sobs, only to bring back the anger. "This place is a madhouse! If you do not find my knife, I quit! The older man stormed from the room.

No sooner had Loralin taken a deep breath to recenter herself than the double doors to the inn flew open and Mr.

Graves came in, pale and out of breath. Call 911. Please. Penny Carlisle needs help in the parking lot!"

Loralin pulled out her phone and called emergency services as she, Tony, and Devin ran to the parking lot to see if they could help. A few more people trailed after them. "Oh God," she whispered as they came upon the scene. Penny was lying next to a Cadillac with something sticking out of her back. Blood was everywhere.

"The poor girl was stabbed," Wanda gasped. "Who would do such a thing? Penny was a mess, but she was a good girl."

"Devin, I don't feel so well," Loralin cried in a whispered tone.

"Whoa," he returned, wrapping his arm around her as her body sagged against him. "It's okay."

"Maybe she's still alive," came a voice from the group that had gathered.

Tony, who was a first aid instructor in his spare time, walked over to Penny, avoiding the blood and her dropped phone. It didn't take long for him to register no pulse and shake his head. The head housekeeper was dead.

"How the hell does something like this happen?" Loralin said softly with a look at Devin. "And right here in my parking lot."

"I don't know, I really don't know" was all he could say as he slowly shook his head.

"We need to find out," Loralin said, straightening herself. "Where is that ambulance and the police?"

Within seconds, the sound of sirens pierced the air, and a car with blue and red lights on the dashboard came to a screeching halt only feet from the two. Miles Robbins, one half of the town's only detective team, and the poster boy for the sexy cop with a dad bod, stepped out. His gaze settled on Loralin.

"Does anyone know what happened?"

Almost everyone in the crowd started talking at once. Detective Robbins looked around and whistled loudly. "Quiet down, everyone. You'll get a chance to talk eventually. "Loralin, can I speak to you first?"

Loralin walked over to her ex-husband, and they hugged. "Miles, this is Devin. Devin, this is my ex-husband."

"Nice to finally meet you," the older man said with a smile.

"Uh, yeah, it's nice to finally meet you, too, sir."

"Just call me Miles," the detective said with a chuckle. "Can you two tell me anything about what happened?"

As the crime scene was secured, Devin and Loralin took turns telling what happened from the time Chef Pierre threw his fit until Miles arrived on the scene. "I just don't know why," Loralin whispered. "We've got to find out who did this to poor Penny."

"My partner and I will find out, Loralin. You need to stay out of it this time. You're not the detective's wife anymore, and this murder was committed on your property."

Loralin nodded to her ex-husband, then turned to go stand by the rest of the gathered crowd. They talked amongst themselves while Miles did what he does. Soon, everyone was told to head back to the inn and stay put until after the scene was examined and cleared.

"What in hell is all the commotion?" came a bark from Chef Pierre.

"We found your knife," Loralin murmured. "I'm not so sure you're going to want to use it again, though."

"What on earth do you mean?" The old chef hadn't looked past them yet.

All Loralin had to do was point, and Chef Pierre dropped

to the ground in a dead faint. Luckily, the paramedics were already there.

7

Closed For Business

Loralin put up a closed sign in the window of her newly opened inn. "This really sucks. People aren't going to want to stay in the murder inn."

"Or, all the customers are only going to want to stay here," Devin said, coming up behind her. "It all depends on how we spin it when this is all done and gone."

Loralin sighed and turned to hug her best friend. "I know you're right, but… poor Penny. She was starting over after a messy divorce. Her only child just started high school. I just can't even imagine."

"What?" Devin hadn't been paying attention, and Loralin followed his gaze."

Miles Robbins was looking at Devin with narrowed eyes, and Loralin shot him a look. Who she hugged was no longer his business. And he was one of the few people who had believed that the pair were just friends. "Don't let him intimidate you, Dev. He's just super protective of me and the girls still. I'm sure you two will be best friends before you know it." Devin gave her a look but didn't say anything. She knew that meant that he was thinking about something. She just had no idea what.

"Loralin, darling, could I trouble you for someplace quiet to question these people?" Miles approached after she and Devin pulled apart, but the older man seemed to be keeping a close eye on the situation.

"Sure. You can use my office. I suppose I should get some food and drinks for these grumpy people." Loralin suddenly felt dead tired and hated the thought of having to move.

"And I should find other accommodations for today's new reservations that will be misplaced tonight," Devin said, turning to leave. "We had three parties checking in today and three checking out."

When the young man walked away, Miles pulled Loralin alongside him. "The refreshments can wait. I'm questioning you first."

"I've already told you everything I know," she said as he made himself comfortable in her chair. "And, you took notes."

"Oh, this isn't about the case, sweetheart. This is about you and your 'best friend.'" The last two words he spoke were emphasized by air quotes.

"Don't call me sweetheart, Miles. We've been divorced for five years, and my best friend is none of your business."

"Like hell he's not! I defended you to our daughter and almost everyone in town. And here you are hanging all over him in front of everyone!"

"First off, I haven't really taken Devin to town, and second, I'm not hanging all over him. It's not my fault he's more affectionate than you ever were." With that, Loralin stormed out of the room and headed for the kitchen. Her guests were getting hungry and thirsty, and she would make sure that was taken care of. To hell with Miles and his stupid jealousy.

***

By the time Miles and his crew were done questioning everyone, it was nearly dinner time. All of the guests were gathered in the lobby, so Loralin took the opportunity to speak.

"Can I have your attention?" she hollered and stood on a bench in the middle of the room. "I want to personally apologize for any inconvenience this has caused you. Because some of you must stay longer than you planned. I want to say that any extra days will be free of charge. The dining room will be open for your convenience. And I would like to offer one free excursion to every room. The inn is closed to new customers, but we still want you to enjoy yourself while you are here. Thank you, everybody. Dinner will begin in 20 minutes.

"Loralin," Miles said, motioning her over. "Thank you for the use of your office."

"You're welcome. So, do you have any suspects yet? Is there anything I can do to make sure the rest of the staff and guests are safe?"

"No suspects yet. But this seemed to be a crime of passion, so I highly doubt it was random. And that, my dear, is all you're going to get on this case unless I feel it is necessary to tell you more.

She shot him a look. "Fine! But I am not your dear! Goodbye, Miles. I'll assume you can find your way out."

"I thought you guys were still good friends," Devin said, walking up behind her. "Would you like to have dinner here?"

"I just want to go home, Dev. The night crew and new security guards are capable of handling things for a bit. And

Miles and I are still friends, but he was acting like a jealous buffoon today."

"Jealous?" he questioned. "Of me?"

"Yep. Now let's go home and..."

"Loralin! Loralin! Where do you think yer going?" For some reason, today, Catherine's voice seemed to grate on her even more than normal.

"I'm going home for dinner," she said, looking at her nemesis. "You guys are welcome to join us. I'm just going to make a salad and some potatoes and throw some steaks on the grill."

The cranky woman completely ignored her. "How do we know we will be safe? I demand ya let us stay at your place."

Loralin knew her fuse was about to blow after the long, horrific day they'd just had, so she grabbed Devin's hand and squeezed for strength. "You are not staying at my home anymore, Catherine. You are perfectly safe here. We've hired security for every floor and the front and back doors. Now, if you'd like to join us for dinner, you are more than welcome. But you *will* be coming back here after." With that, she turned and walked toward the front entrance.

"Bitch!" Catherine said quietly.

"I heard that!" Loralin said as she breezed out the door with Devin at her side.

8

The Sleuth Returns

For the first time in a couple of days, Loralin woke up alone in her bed. After dinner, and forcing Catherine to go back to the inn, she and Devin had been too worn out to watch a movie or talk. They'd both gone straight to bed. She hadn't even had a chance to enjoy the fresh, clean sheets her cleaning lady had put on. She didn't even register the warmth of the down comforter that swallowed her small frame every time she climbed into bed. It was lights out from the moment her head hit the soft cloud she called a pillow.

Once she'd taken stock of the room around her, the memory of what had happened to poor Penny took over. It looked like she'd be taking on the role of head housekeeper for a while until she could bear to replace the best housekeeper in Elk River, if anyone would even want the job at that point. For all she knew, everyone would think they'd be killed if they took the job.

Once she was showered and dressed in a Robbins' Nest Inn t-shirt, she made a call to the night clerk whom Devin was supposed to relieve within the hour. "Robbins' Nest Inn, this is Gage speaking. How may I direct your call?"

'Hey, Gage, it's Loralin. How are things going?"

"Things are great. We have people signing up for off-site excursions and heading to breakfast. It's almost like nothing happened."

"Well, that's good for business, I guess, but it's a sad commentary on humanity." Loralin wished she could forget what happened. But the vision of sweet, scatterbrained Penny lying on the pavement with a giant knife in her back would haunt her for a long time. "Has Maureen come in yet?"

"Yes, ma'am. She's right here. Hold on just a sec."

"Loralin, how are you?" Maureen was the person after Devin who had the most experience in front desk operations. Eventually, she wanted to make her assistant manager.

"I'm as good as can be expected. Look, Devin and I are going to be a little late this morning. Could you hold down the fort for a while?" Loralin wanted to take Devin with her when she went to talk to Miles. She'd been angry the day before, but now she wanted to make sure he knew that they were truly just friends. She kind of liked having her ex on her side. Just because they hadn't liked being married to each other didn't mean they couldn't get along. Even now that their kids were grown, they needed to stick together for their two beautiful daughters.

"Of course. Take your time and do what you've got to do. We'll be fine here."

Now all Loralin had to do was let her new roomie know that he was coming with her. Speaking of the devil, as soon as she hung up the phone, a freshly showered and shaved Devin came into the kitchen and grabbed a coffee cup. "Morning," he grumbled.

"Morning. You might want to grab one of my to-go cups from that cupboard over there. We have a mission this morning."

Devin's eyebrow quirked. "I don't think I like the sound of that. A mission sounds like we are going to be getting into mischief."

"No, not trouble. Maybe think of it as an adventure." Her voice betrayed her. It was supposed to sound serious, but excitement bubbled out.

"And that's better?" he asked, putting the lid on the to-go cup. "What exactly is this adventurous mission we are going on?"

"I want to set things straight with Miles." She paused and gathered her things off the counter.

"And?" he prompted as he followed her to the door.

"And I'm going to see what I can learn about the case."

"Loralin," Devin warned. "He said to stay out of it."

*****

Making their way to the parking lot on the other side of the inn, they walked side by side. Loralin couldn't wait until the concrete dried on her driveway so she could park close to the house again. "I know he did. But truthfully, I just can't. I've got to find out what happened and well…" Another pause as Loralin nodded and waved to some guests who were off to do some horseback riding at a nearby guest ranch.

"Oh, God. Well, what, Loralin?"

"Well, truthfully, I helped Miles solve so many cases that I'm not really sure how he'll do by himself. Right after our divorce, when we weren't talking much, it took him two years to solve a simple theft case."

"Right. So, what you're telling me, now, after we've known each other for years, is that you are one of those old ladies who solves crimes by annoying the whole town with questions and snooping?"

"Rude!" she huffed, climbing into the driver's seat of her SUV. "I'm not old!"

Devin was grinning as he climbed in beside her. "So... you're offended that I called you old but not snoopy and annoying?"

Loralin just had to smile, too. "Okay, I can be a little passionate about crime. Why do you think I married Miles? He looked okay in a uniform, but I loved bouncing ideas off of him and solving problems or questions. And now I have a new partner."

"Oh hell no, Loralin. I'm not going to help you annoy everyone in town." Devin looked genuinely worried. She'd never seen his brow wrinkle quite like that before. "I want people to like me. Especially people I work with and serve at the inn."

"Fine, I'll do the sleuthing, and you just be my sounding board." The puppy dog eyes she was famous for giving him just had to work. "Please?"

"I'll think about it," he finally grumbled before turning to look out the window as the scenery flashed by.

"Good. Now, when we get to the precinct, just play along."

Loralin wasn't quite sure, but she thought she heard him mumble. "Great, I'm going to spend the rest of my life in an American prison." He could be so touchy sometimes. But she needed his help on this one. Miles would take too long to solve this crime. She wanted to get her inn back up and running before she died.

*****

The local police building was right smack in the middle of downtown. In fact, Elk River was so small that almost everything was in the small downtown area, including the courthouse and the grocery store. Loralin pulled up in front and put the SUV in park. "Okay, first and foremost, I am here to apologize for my behavior yesterday, and you are here to back me up. Whatever else happens, it's all on me."

"Shit." He mumbled but still followed her into the building. She was pretty sure at this point that he was wondering what else she hadn't told him. The answer to that, however, was nothing. He knew everything else.

The bell over the door rang, and Loralin nodded a hello to the desk sergeant and headed straight for her ex's office. "Miles? Are you busy?"

"Never for you, Loralin. What's up?" He paused a moment and looked at the man standing next to his ex. "Hello, Devin."

"Hello," the younger man said as his best friend propelled him to a seat in front of the detective's desk.

"What do I owe the pleasure? Is this about the case?"

Loralin smiled. "I just wanted to stop by to apologize, Miles, about the way I acted yesterday. And I wanted to reassure you that your defense of me, about Devin, was right. We are just friends. We do deeply care about each other, and I haven't had someone to hug or hold onto in so long…"

Miles cleared his throat and held up his hand to stop her. "I know, and I believe you. I was just in a mood yesterday. There's nothing like starting the day by finding out your mother's best friend's daughter was murdered in your ex-wife's parking lot."

Loralin had forgotten about the connection. "I'm sorry. I had totally blanked it out."

"Thank you."

Loralin stood to leave but sat back down. "Could I ask a favor of you, Miles?"

"Absolutely!"

"My car is making that noise again. I think it might be a loose wire. Could you check it for me?"

Miles stood and headed toward the door. "I'll be right back." He'd always taken care of her cars and probably always would.

"Here, hold this," Loralin said, giving Devin her phone. "We don't have much time."

"Much time for what?" he asked, then shook his head. "Are you seriously going to look at his notes?"

"No, of course not," she said from behind her ex's desk. "I'm going to photocopy them. Now go keep watch."

"Loralin! Stop it right now!" He was standing by the door listening for the bell that would signal Miles coming back. "Put that stuff back and let's go."

Loralin counted ten pages as they came out of the copy machine. Grabbing the originals, she closed the lid quietly and had the pages and pictures back on the detective's desk a good three minutes before he came back in the door. "Was it the wire?"

"Yeah. It's fixed now, though." He was wiping his hands on his handkerchief.

"Oh, thank you, darling," she said, rising out of the chair to hug her ex. "Tell Meredith hello. We'll have to get together for dinner one of these nights."

"I'll tell her," he said, "And I'm not your darling anymore." When the couple looked at him, he was chuckling. "If you can say stuff like that, so can I.

*****

The SUV eased into Loralin's parking spot, and she turned

the engine off. "You mad?" she asked her companion. Neither of them had spoken the whole way home.

"No," he admitted after a minute, "But can you tell me why the hell I had to be there for that?"

"In case he'd argued. I would have needed you to back me up by saying we were just friends."

Devin opened his door and turned to Loralin. "You are a crazy woman."

"Yeah," she admitted. "But you love me."

"Yes, I do. Now let's get to work. Just because the inn's not open doesn't mean there isn't stuff to do."

The couple walked side by side, once again shrouded in silence. Loralin was starting to worry that she'd offended him. But one thing he should know about her by now was that she did what she had to do, no matter what. She always got what she wanted... eventually, at least. "Are you sure you're not mad at me?" she finally asked as they reached the lobby.

"Yes. Honestly, I'm just exhausted, and I have no idea what to expect from day two." He almost looked scared, or maybe it was lost.

"Hey Dev, things are going to be normal again. I promise. Don't let what's happening now color your decisions. Please.

He took her into his arms and squeezed before letting go. "I'm not thinking about leaving, Loralin. I'm just kind of reeling after yesterday. I'll be okay in a bit. Just be patient with me."

"And you with me," she said before heading to the second-floor supply room to check on the crew. She hated cleaning the rooms, but if she had to, she would jump right in. This was her place, and she'd be damned if she would let a murder derail her dream. There was also another reason she wanted to have daily access to rooms, a reason no one else could know.

*****

Loralin walked into her office and slammed the door. Penny had trained the crew so well that she hadn't been needed to help clean rooms. And now, she couldn't snoop. Maybe it was a blessing, though. She wasn't even sure what she was looking for yet. At least now, she would have time to sit and go over Miles's notes.

Leaving her comfortable leather chair, she walked to the door of the office and looked out. Devin was standing at the counter, lost in thought. "Hey, bestie. Grab us a couple of sandwiches and some fries, and meet me back here. We need to discuss some things."

With a long, labored sigh, he turned and looked at his boss. "Work things?"

"Not exactly," she said with a laugh and shut the door on him again.

It wasn't until she heard whispers from the reservation area that she realized how bad what she'd said sounded. Now everyone would be gossiping about them again. Opening the door one more time, she looked out. "That's not what it sounded like, ladies. We are just friends."

"Yes, ma'am," they answered in unison before turning back to their work.

With that crisis hopefully avoided, but probably not completely, she set the papers she'd taken from her ex-husband's office on her desk and spread them out in some sort of order, pictures across the top and notes along the bottom. It was about time to find out what the police thought about this case.

*****

Devin walked into the office, and Loralin immediately assaulted him with whispered words. "Lock the door!"

"Why?" he asked, setting the food on the meeting table in the corner.

"Because I don't want anyone walking in on us looking at this stuff." Instead of making him bring the food over to her, she moved the documents and pictures over to the table where the food was.

"We're really going to do this." It was more of a statement than a question. He was about to accept his fate.

"Yes. Now let's dig in."

The pair sat shoulder to shoulder and started in on their sandwiches. They were both starving after not having breakfast, but eventually, the pictures pulled them in. "What's this?" Devin asked, lifting a picture of the car that Penny had been lying in front of. "The letters A and is that a U written in blood? Strange."

"Yeah," Loralin agreed. "I wonder if she was naming the killer or giving us a hint."

"Maybe. Who or what could AU or AO or whatever the second thing is be?" Devin was about to speak again when Loralin cut him off.

"Oh my god! I've got it." Loralin was so excited that Devin took a moment to study her. It was as if he'd never truly seen her before.

"Well, tell me!" he finally encouraged after he was able to take his eyes off her.

The picture dropped to the table, and she looked at him with a sly grin. "I've just come up with two suspects."

"Umm, how?" Either he missed something, or he just wasn't good at this sleuthing stuff."

"AU, if that's correct," she said. "Her ex-husband's name is Austin, and he is a mean, violent son of a gun. Last I heard, she had a restraining order against him."

"Okay, that's one. Who is the other?" It may have been crazy, but she was pretty sure he was starting to feel the excitement of the chase.

"Our guest, Augustine Graves. He was Penny's sugar daddy about 10 years ago or so. His wife doesn't know about it either. What if he killed Penny to keep his secret?"

"Really? Are you sure?" She could see the doubt in his eyes.

"Yeah, I was a little weary when I first heard the other day, but I checked it out, and it's true."

Devin sat back in his seat and stared at the papers on the table. "So, what now? What if it's AO? Do we go to Miles with this information, or do we go over all these and then take any information we have to him?"

"We go to Miles," she said. "Eventually. I can't think of anyone offhand with AO, but let's not rule it out."

"Oh, God. I don't like the sounds of that." He sighed and rubbed the back of his neck. "When do we go to Miles?"

"After I've talked to the suspects. I mean, the more information we have, the better. Right?"

Devin gathered the remnants of their food and took them to the trash can by Loralin's desk. "So, then what do we do with the rest of the information you stole?"

Loralin looked offended and glared at her partner in crime. "I borrowed them. Sort of. And we can go ahead and go over everything to see if we can find anything else or anyone else we can talk to.

Devin was mumbling to himself when they sat down together again. Loralin was quite amused. "What did you say?"

"Nothing," he said grumpily, snatching another photo from the table. "I wonder how the killer got the knife out of the kitchen?"

"Everybody has access to the kitchen; it's not locked up." Loralin grabbed one of the documents and searched it for the information she needed. "Hell, it could even have been Austin because we have a night manager or clerk on duty, but he spends most of the time in the back if we have no one checking in."

"And of course, Mr. Graves would have access. I saw him talking with Pierre several times about cooking and such. I even saw them go into the kitchen once." Devin looked over at the paper that Loralin had. What's that?"

Loralin handed it to him. "Physical evidence. There were no usable prints on the knife. But there was powder residue. They don't have the test results back on that yet."

"Yeah, so we have two men who have loved Penny and a chef who, as far as we know, didn't know her more than in passing." Devin grabbed a pad of paper and handed it to Loralin. "Your handwriting is more legible than mine. We should write down who we want to talk to and what we need to investigate.

A big smile came across Loralin's face, and she took the notepad and grabbed a pen. "Now you're getting in the spirit."

"God help me," Devin mumbled. "So, we have people with possible motives and access to the knife. Although everyone technically had access.

"Yeah," Loralin said, tapping her pen on the table. "Who else had something against Penny?"

Devin suddenly sat up straight. "Oh, I know. Remember, Lisa Marie and Chloe were heard bashing Penny, both personal and work-related."

"That's right!" Loralin said, writing something on her pad. "They even fought on opening night. I'm not sure what it was about."

"I wasn't able to find out because I got distracted by a broken luggage cart. But I think Lisa Marie has a crush on me, so maybe she'll tell me something."

"Be careful there, tiger," Loralin said with a laugh. "She's an older woman. She might eat you alive."

Devin huffed. "Apparently, I have a thing for older women. If I supposedly seduced you, I can handle Lisa Marie."

"Okay, fine," she relented. "But you better not replace me. Best friends before hoes."

Devin couldn't help but laugh. "I think that's bros before hoes."

"Same thing," Loralin said, picking up the next picture. "Let's see if there is anything or anyone in the crowd that stands out."

Taking turns looking at the picture got them nowhere. There wasn't anything unusual about the crowd that had gathered to see what was going on. "Okay, who isn't there?" Devin asked.

"Well," Loralin said, taking the photo back from him. "Your family, because they didn't want Trevor to see that, which was on purpose."

"Yeah," he said. "And that family who always seems to be looking over their shoulders. Could they have known Penny? Or could someone have been going after them, and Penny got caught in the crossfire?"

Loralin thought about it. "I mean, I guess anything is possible, but as far as I know, they didn't have anything to do with Penny. And Penny shows no resemblance to the wife. It just doesn't feel like an avenue we should pursue yet."

Devin agreed with a nod and picked up the pictures of the blood splatters and trails. "There's something about these pictures that disturbs me, but I can't put my finger on it."

"Ugh, this would be so much easier with tire tracks or something," Loralin groaned.

"Wait! That's it." Devin stood and started pacing. "How did the killer leave the scene? All of the cars in these pictures belong there, and yes, it was dry out, so there are no tire tracks. But that blood trail right there..." He pointed, and Loralin joined to look.

"What about it?"

"I may be stupid, but I know that's not part of the splatter. It's leading away from the body, and it's too neat; not like splatter at all." Devin's finger drew a straight line to the woods that ran along the property parallel to the parking lot and behind the inn. "They must have escaped into the woods."

"Which would mean it could be anyone." Loralin cried. "The back door, which can be reached through the woods, is actually just another entrance from the stables and the pond. There is free access for anyone."

"Loralin, I think we should call Miles. He needs to search the hotel and the grounds." Devin headed to the desk and the phone.

"The hotel was already searched," Loralin reminded her reluctant fellow sleuth.

"They searched rooms and looked in utility areas," he said. "Don't you think maybe they should be a little more thorough? The killer had to have blood on them. The incinerator, the laundry chute, and God knows what else need to be checked before any evidence is gone."

Loralin knew he was right. Miles had done a cursory search of the hotel, looking for the murderer but not for anything else. Her ex-husband was slacking, and she didn't want to be the one to tell him. When her hand reached out to take the phone from Devin, she felt a little bit ill.

9

Take One For The Team

"This is Detective Robbins." He sounded grumpy as he usually did when he answered his work phone.

"Miles, it's Loralin. We need to talk."

"This doesn't sound good. What's going on? Are the girls okay?" The grumpiness vanished to be replaced by concern.

Loralin took a deep breath and started to talk. "Why didn't you do a thorough search of the hotel and property? The blood in the parking lot tells us the killer escaped into the woods, which leads to the back door."

"Loralin Jackson Robbins!" Her feeling of illness got worse. "How do you know which direction the blood drops go? No one has seen any information on the crime scene, and I hardly believe you remember from yesterday."

"That's hardly important, Miles. You need to get the team out here to go over the hotel and the woods before the evidence is ruined."

The line was silent. Loralin was a little worried that calling her ex out on his failings had killed him. But then he started talking. "It is important. But I don't have a team here in Elk

River anymore, and the team in Casper is busy. Half of their guys got food poisoning at an office party. Of course, the state was notified, but I haven't heard a word from them.

She was relieved to hear that it wasn't a mistake on Miles's part. "So, what do we do, just wait? Evidence could be getting erased as we speak."

"I did what I could, Loralin. We searched the rooms and took a cursory look around the rest of the place. If you hadn't noticed, there is still quite a bit of scene tape in your basement and outdoor areas, and the guards were told to look out for anyone in the areas they aren't supposed to be in."

"Okay," Loralin said, rubbing her forehead as her mind worked overtime. "Could Cheyenne dispatch a team?

"Maybe. I haven't called them because, as you know, Don Peterson and I don't get along. He's not going to do a favor for me."

"But he might for me," Loralin said, smiling. "Don always did have a soft spot for me."

"Don't do it, sweetheart. I don't want you having to deal with 'Handsy Don' just so I can get a crime scene processed properly." Sometimes it was nice knowing Miles still cared enough to protect her. But sometimes it was just annoying.

"I'll have a team up here from Cheyenne by this afternoon." Loralin hung up the phone before Miles could object.

"What is that all about?" Devin asked warily. "What are you going to do with this Don character?"

"I'm going to sweet-talk him and perhaps go out with him. And don't you go getting overprotective of me, too. I can handle myself with this man."

Devin slid her desk chair back and raised his hands in the air. "Go for it." He rose from the chair, and Loralin took his place.

*****

The phone rang three times before the pudgy, sweet, but desperate Chief of police answered his personal cell phone. "Loralin Robbins, to what do I owe this honor?"

"Hi Don!" Her voice became sweet and flirty. "I was sitting here looking at my two tickets for the Chase Goldman concert at the event center in Casper, and I remembered you and your friends liked him. Do you know anyone who would want to take one of these tickets off my hands?"

"Oh, Loralin, darlin', you are a sly one. If you wanted a date, all you had to do was ask." The ickiness factor in the room rose by a million. "I think you know I've been sweet on you since I worked alongside that no-good ex-husband of yours in Elk River."

Loralin shivered and tried not to let him hear her gag. "You got me. I need a favor, and if you can grant it to me, we can go on a nice date to the concert and maybe have a late dinner." She felt Devin's hand tighten on her shoulder, and she shook it off. She didn't need to be protected!

"What kind of favor is that, beautiful?" Now his voice was the one that sounded wary.

"Could Elk River borrow your crime scene guys for an afternoon? We had a nasty murder here, and we don't have a team anymore." Her voice dripped with sugar. If she'd been there in person with Don, she'd have been batting her eyelashes at him… and trying not to vomit.

"Well, I don't know. Is your no-good ex in charge of the case?" his voice started to sound slightly defeated.

"Well, yes. But I'll be here. And don't forget the concert and dinner, sweet cheeks." Devin spun Loralin around in her chair and stuck his finger down his throat. They both tried not to laugh.

"Well, I, I suppose we could head up there today. We aren't working on any cases. I'll get everyone together and be there in about two and a half hours."

"Thank you, Don. See you then!" Loralin hung up and leaned back in her chair. "That man is so boring and handsy. But I want this case solved ASAP."

"I hope you know what you're doing," Devin said. "Going out with a man you despise; I don't think I could take one for the team like that."

*****

"So, what now?" Devin asked. "I don't see much else on these papers or in the photographs."

Loralin got up from the table and went to her mini fridge to get them some water. "Yeah, I don't either. At least for now. Maybe there will be something later, but right now I think we should just go talk to people."

Devin once again oozed frustration. "So, we just randomly go up to people and start asking them questions?"

Loralin laughed. "Not exactly. For example, if I need to talk to Chef about something that is a regular part of running the inn, I will work it into the conversation."

"Okay, I can see how that works. Are you going to call this Austin character?"

Loralin unlocked her phone and scrolled through the contacts. "The problem is, I don't think I have Austin's number."

"Well, that was short-lived," he said with a sigh. "Someone must have his number."

A knock came on the door. Loralin completely forgot that they had locked it. "Can I help… Hello Miles. Come on in."

The detective looked around the room and settled on the table in the corner. "So that's the scene of the crime?" he grumbled. "I could have you arrested for that."

"I warned her, boss," Devin said with a salute.

"I like this kid. And as for you, Loralin, I need you to stay the hell out of this. I can handle it."

Loralin rolled her eyes at her ex. "I'm sure you can. But if I help you, it will get done faster. This is killing my dream, Miles."

"Fine." He seemed to be giving in. "Tell me what you've got, and then you can stay the hell out of it. "I'll do it as quickly as I possibly can."

Devin knew Loralin well enough to know that she wouldn't give in that easily. "We wanted to check on Penny's ex, Austin. You know, the AU wrote in blood on Mr. Grave's car."

"Well, I can tell you where Austin is," Miles said with a shrug. "He's been in jail in Casper for the last three weeks and will most likely be sent to the state pen for a few years."

Loralin felt disappointment wash over her. It would have been so easy if it were the violent ex-husband whose initials were written in blood by the victim. But she still had hope that it might be Mr. Graves or even Chef Pierre. She wasn't about to tell Miles that. Yet. It all depended on what she found out. And as luck would have it, she had a meeting with the chef in just a few minutes. "I'm going to have to get out of here. I have some meetings to attend to."

"I'll leave you to it," Miles said, turning to the door. "But I mean it, Loralin. Stay out of this case, or I will have you arrested."

Devin chuckled as the detective walked out and shut the door. "I think he's serious."

"He would never arrest me. He just likes threatening it."

Devin shook his head and followed Loralin out. "I sure hope so."

"Come on," Loralin said with a laugh of her own. "I'll show you how it's done."

*****

Chef Pierre was sitting at a table in the dining room, planning out next week's menu, when the two friends arrived. He invited them to sit and put his papers away. "We had two line cooks quit because of the murder."

"Great," Loralin sighed. "I have a pool of applicants that I'll go through to find you replacements as soon as possible."

"I can't believe they quit because of the murder," Devin said. "It didn't happen in the kitchen, and it wasn't related to anything involving this part of the inn."

"That we know of," Loralin said quietly. "How well did you know Penny, Pierre?"

"In passing," he said with a wave of his hand. "I've seen her around town but never really talked to her. I feel bad for the girl, but she had nothing to do with me."

Devin took his cue from Loralin. It seemed he could tell where she wanted to go with the questioning. "I wonder if anyone else here at the inn had a problem with her."

"I'd heard something about the other housekeepers," Loralin said. "I saw part of it but don't know what it was about."

"Those three are so catty when you get them together," Pierre said with a rolling of eyes. "They were fighting over who had to clean the men's bathroom. Once that Penny girl left, the other two talked about how they should toss her in the river."

Devin sat back in the chair and looked at Loralin. "That poor girl indeed. It seems she didn't have any real enemies. I don't envy Miles in having to solve it."

"Oh, you never know," Loralin said, returning his look. "I've heard of people murdering for less than a bad job assignment.

Chef Pierre grunted. "I have more enemies than that girl. I guess I should consider myself lucky that someone didn't turn my knife on me."

The three co-workers sat and contemplated how someone with no real enemies ended up dead with a knife in their back in the parking lot of the local inn.

Loralin and Devin went their separate ways after the meeting with the chef. She wanted to get busy to hire some more line cooks, and Devin wanted to check with the desk clerk about reservations for the upcoming month. God willing, they'd only be closed for another couple of days.

Guests were milling around the lobby with cups full of free but flavorful coffee. All on-site excursions were canceled until further notice, so people were spending their time reading and visiting in the seating areas near the main entrance.

Just after two p.m., the main doors opened, and a group of men and women paraded in. The guests in the lobby became quiet and stared. Devin picked up the phone and dialed his boss. "Loralin, the crime scene people are here. I think they scared the guests."

"I'll be right out." She hurried from the office and rushed to the front of the lobby. "Ladies and Gentlemen, these people are here to finish up the investigation of the crime scene from yesterday. Please feel free to continue to have fun, but also please stay out of their way. The sooner they finish up, the sooner we can all get back to normal. Thank you."

Chief Don Peterson approached Loralin, and Devin swooped in to act as a buffer. "Loralin, my dear," the older man said, taking her hand and pressing a kiss to the back of it. "What a pleasure. It seems we met up with the state crew on the road. My guys will take the inn, and they will take the woods and surrounding areas."

Loralin fought the urge to pull her hand away from him and wipe it on her jeans. "That sounds fine, Don. Please inconvenience my guests as little as possible. We've already had a rocky start."

"Yes, ma'am. I've informed my team." The handsome man now standing behind Don winked as he broke in on their conversation. "Hello, ma'am. What a great place you have here. My name is Damien Pacer. I'm the head of the state crime scene investigators."

"It's, it's uh nice to meet you," Loralin stammered, gazing into his ocean-blue eyes. How had she not known that the head of the state CSI team was so damn good-looking?

"We will be out of your hair as soon as possible, ma'am." And then he was gone, walking back out the main entrance to join his team outside.

"Could you have been more obvious?" Devin mumbled as he pulled his best friend away from the people gathered around.

Loralin touched her long brown hair and straightened her shirt. "I don't know what you mean. Obvious about what?"

"You have the hots for the State guy. You practically choked on your tongue trying to talk to him."

Loralin didn't like his tone of voice. "And what's wrong with that? You sound like Miles. You aren't my ex-husband, and you aren't my boyfriend, so stop acting like you are!" She stomped away.

"Someone's a little touchy today," Tony said as he polished the nearby counter.

"Yeah," Devin said softly. "Stress." He didn't feel like explaining anymore; he just went after her.

"Loralin!" He was annoyed to see that she kept walking. "Loralin Robbins, I'm trying to apologize, will you slow down!"

She finally stopped and turned to him. "Why did you act like that? You aren't jealous, are you?"

Devin looked like he'd been slapped. "Ha! Jealous? No. Why would I be jealous? That guy was so full of himself, he probably doesn't know what a best friend is."

Loralin looked at Devin and searched his expression. She'd often wondered if he'd had a crush on her, but always ruled it out. It wasn't like him to act like that. But, then again, he had never seen a guy hit on her in person either. He was probably just being protective. "It's okay," she finally said, giving him a big hug. "All of this is just so stressful and annoying. Once the crime scene people leave, would you and your family have dinner with me?"

"Sure," he said with his big, bright smile. "Do you want to go out or eat here at the inn?"

"Let's go out," she said with a sly grin. "Let's see if we can get your mother to behave in public."

Devin laughed and let her go. "I'll see you soon."

10

Fingerprints & Family Drama

Loralin, Devin, and his family piled into her SUV for the quick drive into town, where they pulled up in front of a local landmark. Maybell's diner had been in business, with Maybell at the helm, for as long as anyone could remember. The previous year, when Maybell had passed away, her daughter Marissa had taken over.

"Well, howdy, Loralin," Marissa said. "How many in your party today?"

"There will be five of us," she said. "Could we have a table somewhere in the back?"

The beautiful proprietor, who was beginning to look much like her mother, grabbed a stack of menus and led the way to a table for six at the back of the restaurant. "I'll send Latisha right out to get your order."

"So, how has everybody been doing since the incident yesterday?" Loralin asked as she perused the menu.

"Look at ya!" Catherine said, "She can't even call it what it was. Some poor girl was murdered right on your property."

Loralin felt Devin tense up beside her. "I know exactly what it was," she gritted out. "But it is much less disturbing to the younger one and others here around us if we don't call it what it really is."

Devin's mother had the good sense to look embarrassed at the fact that she'd forgotten that her young son was with her. Her face reddened a bit, and she looked down.

Mark put his menu down and looked around the table. "To hear it told," he began. "Folks around the inn have said you're something of an amateur detective, Loralin."

She shrugged and set her menu down, too. "I used to run scenarios and what-ifs with my ex-husband. I came up with a good idea now and then that may or may not have helped get a case or two solved."

"So who do ya think did this?" Catherine asked. "From what I hear, yer housekeeper was well-liked."

"She was," Devin confirmed. "There isn't much info on the case yet. All we know is that the ex-husband was ruled out, and it will be a few days before any forensic answers are available."

Loralin sent her best friend a smile of thanks. She was beginning to think she'd made a mistake in wanting to see if Catherine could behave herself. Luckily, the waitress came, and the conversation switched to drink and food orders.

*****

"I'm so glad to see that the food hasn't changed any since Maybell passed away," Loralin said as she took a bite of her chicken-fried steak. "She has the best down-home cooking in Wyoming."

"What happened to her?" Catherine said with an air of arrogance. "Did your damn inn kill her, too?"

"Mother!" Devin reprimanded. "That's enough!" Catherine rolled her eyes and looked back at her plate.

"The food is wonderful," Mark agreed. "It kind of reminds me of my nan's cooking."

"Well, hello there, folks!" Wanda, her sister Thelma, and Henry were being led to a table nearby. "I see you decided to take a break from the inn and have some of Maybell's wonderful food."

"Yes," Loralin said, returning the woman's kind smile. "I'm sorry if the inn is getting boring. We hope to open back up fully by tomorrow sometime."

As Wanda made her way to their table, she turned back. "Loralin, could I talk to you for a moment over here?"

Loralin looked at Devin and shrugged her shoulders. "I'll be right back. When she reached Wanda's table, she was asked to have a seat.

"I have some questions about the..." the woman moved in close and whispered, "murder!"

Henry was gentleman enough to hold a chair out for Loralin, and she sat. "What's up, Wanda? I don't know much about it."

"Nonsense, dearie," the older woman said with a chuckle. "You know everything in town. Do they have any suspects? I just can't imagine who would kill Penny. She was a bit wild but a good girl."

Loralin looked over at Devin, giving him a pleading look. It seemed he didn't know what she was trying to say. "Well, I don't think they have any suspects yet. Most of the forensic evidence is just now heading to processing."

The woman tsked. "That ex-husband of yours is as slow as molasses. Didn't questioning people give them anyone to look at? I mean, even I was questioned, and I wasn't there. I'd spent the night with Thelma and Henry. We even had breakfast here at Maybelle's."

"Well, you know," Loralin said politely as she shot Devin another look. "They had to question everybody who was staying at or working at the inn."

"I suppose so," the older woman relented. "And today they took fingerprints. It took forever to get that feeling of yuck off my fingers."

"Loralin," Devin said as he approached. He'd finally gotten the hint. "I'm sorry, folks. May I have my boss back? It's time to order dessert."

"Have a great night," Loralin said, getting up from her chair and following Devin. "Well, Wanda has an alibi. Not that she was ever a suspect in my eyes, though."

"What, are you two telling secrets about?" Catherine said with disgust. "Probably making plans to fu…"

"Catherine!" Mark said, pointing to their younger son. "I swear you're losing your mind more and more every day. Thank goodness we're going home soon. I think this American air has affected your brain."

Wife glared at husband, but no other words were exchanged as the waitress came back to take dessert orders. Loralin was frustrated with her best friend's mother. She'd become so one-dimensional. When Devin spent time on the phone with Heather, she was almost sweet and was making plans to get the two together in the same place. When Loralin had entered the picture, she'd become obsessed. All she ever thought about anymore was keeping them from being a couple, from doing the things couples do. No matter what anyone did or said could get her away from that one topic. She seemed to dwell on it day and night. Had she broken her best friend's mother?

At least Loralin was somewhat satisfied with the investigation. They had two people ruled out, and the intensive search was probably just wrapping up at the inn. Now she just had to find a way to get the forensic information from her ex-husband.

11

Forensics & Dinner Dates

The inn was allowed to reopen after a thorough cleaning. Everyone was back at work the day after the forensic teams took all of their possible evidence to the state lab.

It seemed that Devin had been correct about the popularity of the place soaring. After some initial cancellations, more due to the unknown reopening date than the murder itself, people were calling in from all over trying to get reservations.

Loralin had wanted her inn to be popular, but she hoped she was ready for all the lookie-loos that would invade the space. And Chef Pierre was just starting the new line cooks she'd hired. Hopefully, they would rise to the occasion as the hotel was booked solid for several weeks.

Loralin walked into the kitchen where Devin sat reading the paper. "Good morning."

"I sure hope so. It's going to be our first day back at an open inn. I think I'm going to make my move and see what I can get out of Lisa Marie."

"Make your move?" Loralin asked, pouring a cup of coffee

and sitting next to her best friend.

"Yeah. I don't see anything wrong with going on a date with a beautiful woman."

"You do realize this beautiful woman is forty years old, right?" Why was she so opposed to him dating Lisa Marie? Any other woman, she'd be fine with. Well, maybe not any other woman but someone special.

"I do. There isn't a law against it. And she is very beautiful." The look on his face was one of excitement that had Loralin wondering if this was just an information-finding date or if he really had a thing for Lisa Marie.

"Okay then. Good luck. I hope she feels the same… I guess." Loralin got up and put her coffee cup in the sink. "I'm going to take a drive up to Cheyenne to see our friend Don. Maybe a kiss on his chubby little cheek will result in him sharing forensic information with us when it's time."

Devin joined her at the sink and put his hand on her shoulder. "I hate that you have to do that. Can't you steal them again from Miles?"

Loralin patted his hand. "It's fine, Dev. I don't mind. And I can't do the photocopy thing again. Miles will be very careful from now on."

"Are you sure? I could come with you and work on Lisa Marie tomorrow." Loralin appreciated that he was worried about her.

"I'm sure," she said with a reassuring smile. "And you need to stay here to manage the hotel. We can't both be gone all day."

"Okay," he relented. "Drive safe, and I'll see you this evening." He headed for the front door and the path that led to the inn.

*****

The morning had been busy, and Devin hadn't had much time to breathe, let alone get Lisa Marie alone to ask her out. But now that it was time for the woman's lunch break, he figured he could make the time to talk to her.

The employee break room was thankfully empty except for the woman he needed to talk to. "Hey, Lisa Marie. How are you?"

"Oh, hi Devin. I'm good, how are you?" Her smile lit up her whole face, and the bun she kept her neat, dark hair in was actually kind of sexy.

"I'm good. It's been so boring the last few days, and Loralin hasn't been up to going out."

"Really? That's such a shame. I love going out to the bar on County Road between Elk River and Boone." Her smile told him that he was about to score a date.

"That sounds amazing. Would you perhaps like to show me the nightlife one of these days?" He turned his smile on her this time and saw her blush.

"I'd love to. How about tonight?"

Devin felt like jumping for joy. He was in with her, and now all he had to do was enjoy himself while getting info from one person who had access to areas of the hotel that most others didn't. "I'll meet you in the lobby at 6?"

"I'll be there, gorgeous." She practically purred. Damn, this was going to be fun. He didn't think they'd have much in common, but he was due for a fun night with a beautiful woman.

*****

Loralin hated the two-and-a-half-hour drive to Cheyenne because it was so boring. It wasn't bad if she had someone to talk to, but today she was all alone. When the large brick

City building that housed Don's office loomed ahead of her, she relaxed. At least now she would have something to occupy her mind. The whole trip, thoughts that she didn't like at all bombarded her, and no matter how hard she tried, she couldn't get rid of them. They were disturbing thoughts, and the sooner she got rid of them, the better.

Luckily, she found a parking spot quickly and was inside within minutes. "I'm here to see Don Peterson."

The man at the desk looked like he was permanently irritated at the human race. "And who are you?"

Loralin held her tongue at his rudeness. She wanted this day to go smoothly. "Loralin Robbins."

"Is he expecting you?" The man took a moment to blow his nose loudly on a handkerchief.

"Well, no. But I'm sure he'll see me. Just give him my name."

Apparently, she was standing too close to the counter because the man picked up the phone receiver and moved away, turning his back on her. He had barely hung up when Don Peterson was standing behind her, waiting for her to turn.

"Loralin! What a pleasant surprise."

"Don, it's so good to see you. How have you been?"

"I just saw you yesterday, and not much has changed," he said hesitantly. "Is everything okay?"

Loralin kicked herself for getting a bit overzealous in her attempt to get Don to do what she wanted. She needed to slow down and back off again. "Sorry, Donnie. I'm just a little overwhelmed from the last few days. Is there someplace we can talk privately?"

The man's face lit up brighter than a spotlight on a New York stage. "Let's go to my office," he said. Loralin had never heard something so creepy. His hands were just itching to touch her, and she made a mental note to stay a safe distance away from him whenever possible.

Once they were settled in his office with Don behind his desk and Loralin in a chair in front of it, she felt much better. "I'm just going to get right to the point. I have a favor to ask."

"I'll help if I can, Loralin. What do you need?" His eyes never left her. His gaze was what he most likely thought was smoldering, but to her, it just looked creepy.

"Miles has told you how I am with his cases, right?" She knew he had. The two men used to be friends a long, long time ago.

"Everyone in every law enforcement office in the state knows," he joked. "So, what I'm getting is that you need me to leak you information on the forensics of the case because Miles is too much of an ass to let you help him investigate."

She always felt the need to defend her ex, even if it wasn't in her best interest. "Well, technically, I shouldn't help him investigate the case. But you know how I am. I just have to be in the know. Especially since it involves my inn."

Don sat back in his chair and templed his hands. "So, what are you willing to do in return?"

This was the part she hadn't thought about much. Would he want another date or one of her famous apple pies or something more, like a night spent with her... God forbid. "I, I don't know. Is there something you wanted?"

Don got that creepy grin on his face again, and Loralin's heart dropped to her feet. Were her hands shaking? "I'll tell you what. Since we already have that concert date planned, I'm going to do this for nothing in return."

This was not like Don at all. He was not only a slimy man, but he was a greedy one, too. "I'm a bit confused."

"It's simple, Loralin. With as much as I'm fond of you, the one thing I want most in this world is to one-up your ex-husband. Just make sure that he knows that any info you 'come upon' was courtesy of me."

Loralin had to stop herself from laughing. As much as she liked her ex, he was the one who had started the rift with Don. He kind of deserved anything he got. "So, we have a deal then." Her hand reached out to shake.

"We have a deal," Don said, slipping his hand into hers. "Allow me to show you out."

It didn't come as a surprise to Loralin when she felt his hand swat her ass on the way out. But at this point, she didn't care. She had a new ally. She didn't want to dwell on the fact that it was Handsy Don.

*****

Devin couldn't wait for work to end. He hadn't gone out for drinks and maybe some dancing in a long, long time. It wasn't his scene, but he did enjoy the occasional night out. "Has anyone seen Loralin yet?"

"She just walked in," Tony said, pointing to the door.

When Devin looked up, he smiled. She seemed happy with what she'd done that day. When she motioned to her office, he nodded and headed that way. Once they were both inside, he finally spoke. "So, how did it go?"

"Whatever we need to know, we will know." She was so proud of herself for going through with the plan.

"And what did it cost you?" He was dreading her answer. If that stupid little man so much as laid a hand on her…"

"Absolutely nothing. How did things go with Lisa Marie?" She sat down at her desk and put her feet up. She still hated the drive to Cheyenne, both ways.

"Wait a sec," Devin said more as a question than a statement. "You didn't have to give him a second date or anything?"

"Nope," she said with a laugh. "He just wants to be able to one-up Miles."

Devin chuckled and took a seat in front of her desk. "Well, I have a date tonight. With one Lisa Marie Winchell. We are going to the bar on County Road for some drinks and dancing, and I hope for some information exchange."

"Mmm Hmm," Loralin said with a grin. "Are you sure it will be information you're exchanging?"

"Strictly," Devin emphasized. "She's beautiful, and I can't wait to have a fun evening, but she's not my type."

"Okay," Loralin said in a sing-song voice. "I guess we'll find out. What are your parents doing tonight? Do I have to entertain them?"

"Nope. They are going to dine here in the hotel and make an early night of things. They plan on going on the excursion to Casper tomorrow."

With a nod, Loralin removed her feet from the desk and stood. "When is your date?"

Devin took his phone out of his pocket and looked at the time. "Actually, I have to meet her in the lobby in five minutes. I'll see you at home tonight."

"Yeah," Loralin said as she walked to the door with her best friend. "Have fun and be careful."

Devin swore he saw something like anger or frustration in her eyes.

*****

Devin had run home to change clothes after he'd made the date. Wearing his work clothes to a bar wouldn't have been good, especially the bulky Robbins' Nest Blazer. Stepping out of his boss's office, he smiled at Lisa Marie as she stood by the check-in counter waiting for him. She sure cleaned up well. Her bun was gone, and her hair cascaded down around her shoulders. Her makeup was refreshed, and she was wearing a black skirt with a flowy white top. She looked amazing. "You look beautiful," he said, putting a kiss on her cheek."

"You don't look so bad yourself," she said, leaning into the kiss. "It's no wonder Loralin snatched you up."

Devin didn't like how she'd put that. Loralin hadn't snatched him up. He was still very single. "We're just...."

"Best friends, I know." Lisa Marie said with a smirk. "I sure hope you're right. I don't want to lose my job for going out with you."

"You won't," Devin assured her as he ushered her out of the building and toward the parking lot. "She sees who she wants, and I see who I want, and we meet back at her place to gossip about it."

Lisa Marie laughed. "Remind me to watch what I say."

The drive to the Bar was surprisingly quick. It was in the opposite direction from the main part of town. "We may do things differently in Australia, but what good is having a bar out here in the middle of nowhere?"

"Well, there are a couple of reasons," she stated as she drove in the dim light of dusk. "First, things can get wild and crazy and loud, and it doesn't bother anyone in town or the residential areas. And second, this road leads from Boone to Elk River, kind of a back route. This way, the bar not only picks up locals but also travelers and people from the nearby towns. It's a win-win for everyone."

"Okay, that makes sense." Devin was so relieved that Lisa Marie was a careful driver. He was still a bit nervous in cars since the damn Americans drove on the wrong side of the road. "Does this place have food? I should have invited you to dinner first."

"Oh, boy, are you in for a treat!" Lisa Marie said with excitement. "The bar on County Road is known for its hot wings, chicken strips, burgers, and freshly made home fries."

"Good. I'm starving. When do we get there?"

"It's right around the curve." Lisa Marie smiled at him and then turned back to the road. "I think this is going to be a fun evening."

Devin was not having a bad time. Lisa Marie was an amazing conversationalist, and the smells coming from inside the kitchen were making him even hungrier. "Thanks for recommending this beer. I just really don't know much about American beer."

"You like it, huh? It's my favorite, a local microbrew."

Devin was about to comment, but the waiter brought their dinners, and they both remained quiet for a bit. She'd been right, the food was phenomenal. It would almost have been a crime to speak while eating it. It was meant to be thoroughly enjoyed with no interruptions.

"How are you adjusting to American food?" Lisa Marie finally asked. "My cousin spent years in Australia and never really did come to like the food differences."

"It's good," he relented. "Hell, sometimes, like tonight, it's great. But man, I do miss a good meat pie sometimes."

"Ask Loralin to make you one. She's an amazing cook."

"So, how do you know Loralin?" he asked, pushing his plate away. When he looked into her eyes, something short-circuited in his brain for just a second. He could go swimming in her ocean-blue eyes. And he could smack himself for being so corny.

"I worked at her grandparents' inn for many years until it shut down ten years ago." Devin could tell it was a good memory for her. "I remember when I heard that Loralin was reopening it. I was the first person to apply."

"Even before Penny, huh?"

Lisa Marie chuckled. "Yeah, at the time, Penny was happy with her job. But her boss can be an ass, so I convinced her to apply at Robbins' Nest."

"Oh, okay. Were you mad that she got head of housekeeping?" He wouldn't blame her if she were. But it would also be kind of a motive. He prayed that it wasn't the case.

"Oh hell no," she said quickly. "You couldn't pay me to do that job anywhere. Did it once, won't ever do it again."

Devin felt an immense sense of relief. The longer he spent with this beautiful woman, the more he wanted to know her. He would be so upset if she turned out to be a murderer. "I get it. That is one job in a hotel that I hate doing, and to be managing everyone who is doing it is just a pain in the ass."

"I don't think I could be an owner or a manager either," Lisa Marie put in. "The stress would kill me. Just like when Penny quit her other job, and her boss freaked out. He yelled at her in public and even threatened to make her pay for going to the competition. She was damn good at her job, and it was stressful for him to lose her."

Devin couldn't help but chuckle. He could sympathize with the old man. Losing good workers was the pits. "Has anyone told the police about this guy? It sounds like a motive to me."

Lisa Marie looked at him thoughtfully. "You know, I'm not sure. They didn't question Chloe and me much because we were each other's alibi. We were here until last call that night."

"Well, I'm glad you didn't have to be grilled by them. I hear Miles can be a bit rough if he has to." Devin now had some news for Loralin. There was a new suspect that they could focus on. And of course, they still hadn't ruled out Augustine Graves yet. He was trying to remember if there had been any notes from Miles about the two housekeepers being ruled out.

"Miles is a pussy cat. I dated him twice after the divorce. He was a bit too… normal for me, I guess." Lisa Marie's description of Miles seemed to fit him. He was just a normal, calm, everyday guy.

"So that fight between you guys and Penny was nothing?" He knew they had alibis, but he was curious."

"Those arguments were mild in comparison to some of the fights housekeepers get into. None of us likes cleaning bathrooms. And of course, the head housekeeper gets the brunt of it. But we all got along. It really meant nothing."

Devin somehow knew that she was telling the truth. "So, is it too soon after eating to do some dancing?"

"It's never too soon!" she hollered as the live band came on stage to loud applause. "I hope you can line dance."

Devin wasn't sure if this night could get any better, but he couldn't wait to find out.

12

Miles Makes An Arrest

Loralin walked into the kitchen in her bathrobe and looked out the window. She swallowed down a lump in her throat. Devin hadn't come home, and she was worried sick. She felt like crying.

"Loralin! Where are you?" The front door slammed, and the worry melted away. The anger, however, stayed and festered in the thirty seconds it took for him to appear in the kitchen.

"Where the hell have you been?" Halfway through the sentence, the tears welled in her eye, and her voice cracked. "I've been worried sick about you."

"Hey," he said softly. "Are you crying?"

She wiped her eyes. "Does it matter? You were gone all night and didn't call to let me know you wouldn't be home."

Devin pulled her into his arms. "I'm sorry. One thing led to another, and I fell asleep."

Her head was buried in his chest. "Did you sleep with her?" she mumbled.

"Wait a minute," he said, pulling back and searching her expression. "Are you jealous?" They didn't have feelings like that for each other. But he did admit that sometimes it was hard to see her with other people. He wasn't sure what that meant.

"Of course not," she sneered. "I was just worried."

"I don't know. What were you worried about, me having sex with her or me leaving you for her?"

Loralin shrugged and moved to the breakfast nook, where she sat at the window bench. "It always feels like it's the end of us when we are with other people. It's like our bond is so strong and defies definition that it's hard to imagine either one of us with a partner because…"

"Because what?" Devin asked as he sat next to her on the bench.

"Because I don't think anyone else can tolerate our relationship. Remember when I dated Jim? He couldn't handle it. I really liked him, but he demanded that I stop talking to you."

"Yeah, I remember. It was the same when I dated Madison. And truthfully, I didn't like Jim. I felt threatened by him. I guess I thought he'd replace me."

"So, what do we do?" Loralin hoped he had an answer because she sure didn't.

"I don't know. I guess we take it one day at a time and be open about stuff?"

"Yeah, I guess," she agreed. "Are you going out with Lisa Marie again?"

"Yes."

"Okay," Loralin said softly as she got up from the bench. "Maybe it's best if we don't talk much about that."

"Done. But we will have to talk about what I learned last night."

"Oh?" She was now more curious than hurt or angry.

"Yep. I've got a new suspect and a couple that are now ruled out."

Loralin headed for her bedroom. "Meet me in my office at noon. We'll have lunch and talk!"

*****

Devin was standing outside the office door right when the clock on his phone switched to noon. He had two lunch baskets with him. "Knock, knock he said, opening the door. I have lunch and information for my bestest friend in the whole world."

"Come on in," she said with a smile. "I'm starving for food and information."

Devin set up the food at the meeting table, and Loralin brought her notepad and the documents she photocopied from Miles. "Have a seat and let's dig in."

"Okay, so you said we could rule out two possible suspects. Who are they?"

Devin finished chewing his bite of food. "Lisa Marie and Chloe. The fight was just usual stuff between housekeepers, and they were together at the bar until last call. They couldn't have been here during the murder."

Loralin breathed a sigh of relief. "I like those girls, so I'm glad. Now, what about the new suspect? Is it someone associated with the hotel?"

"Nope." Devin continued to eat until Loralin looked like she was about ready to jump out of her skin in anticipation of his explanation. "Did you know that Mr. Matthews from the Roadway Hotel on Route 245 cursed out dear Penny and threatened to ruin her career if she started working for you?"

"Wow," Loralin whispered. "I knew there had been a scene, but I didn't know it was that bad. He was rightfully upset, but has always seemed harmlessly grumpy, not murderous."

"I mean," Devin continued once he pushed his empty food containers away from him. "As far as motives go, it isn't super strong, but before I left her house this morning, Lisa Marie said she'd heard Mr. Matthews was in financial trouble for a while now. Maybe he tried to convince Penny to return after he saw how successful the grand opening was, and things just got out of hand."

"No, because he would have had to steal Chef Pierre's knife." She sat and thought for a while before she came up with a plausible explanation. Okay, what if he was going to use the knife to persuade her, and when it didn't work, he lost control and stabbed her? Maybe the success of the grand opening made him angry, and that's why he grabbed the knife."

"Possibly," Devin agreed. "He came here to spy, but ended up going to desperate measures. He was here, right? I'm not even sure what he looks like."

"Yeah, he was that tall, skinny man with glasses who kept taking notes about everything." Loralin had to think about where all she'd seen him that day. "And I did see him leaving the dining room at close, so he could have grabbed the knife."

"Do we know when Chef first noticed the knife missing?" Devin's mind was working now. He was actually enjoying this mystery stuff.

Loralin picked up one of the documents she'd copied and scanned through the words. "Ah, yeah, right here it says he used it to cook opening night, washed and dried it, and put it in his knife rack. He noticed it was gone the next morning when it wasn't in its usual spot."

"And since the kitchen doors are never locked and the dining room is always open for snacks and drinks… maybe we should give Miles a call and tell him what we've found." For Loralin's sake, Devin hoped this would be the end of things, but for himself, he hoped he would get the chance to snoop some more."

*****

"So, what did he say?" Devin asked when he got back from taking care of another tantrum from Chef Pierre. He'd been gone a half hour, and Loralin hung up just as he walked into the office.

"He's going to go over to the Roadway and talk to Butch Matthews." She was fiddling with the calendar on her desk, a sure sign that she was thinking. "It took me a while to convince him, but then I pointed out that he was just wary because it was coming from me. He then reminded me to stay out of it."

"So, the usual. I hope something comes of this. I want things to feel normal again." He wanted it more for her than for himself. There was no norm for him yet. Things wouldn't start to get normal for him until his parents left.

"Yeah, I guess," Loralin said with a sigh. "I just get a feeling that something is off about him using the knife." She didn't offer more insight into her thoughts.

*****

"When is your date with Lisa Marie?" Loralin asked Devin as they prepared to leave for the day.

"We're going straight to dinner from here. Why?" He looked for any signs that Loralin was uncomfortable with the situation.

"I wasn't sure if you'd be home for dinner. I think I'm going to head over to the Roadway Hotel and deliver a thank-you basket to Butch Matthews for taking on our guests when we were closed down."

"Ah," Devin said with a chuckle. "And to see what damage Miles did while he was there?"

"Yep. Have fun, and I'll see you after your date or in the morning." She picked up her bag and a few file folders and left the office.

Devin was quite glad to see that she seemed to be accepting that he was going out with Lisa Marie. "Are you ready to go?" he asked when he saw his date waiting at the check-in counter.

"I sure am. I thought tonight we would try some Chinese food. We have a local buffet that probably has the best fried dumplings in the state." Her smile made his insides tighten.

"Sounds amazing," Devin said as he put his hand on the small of her back and escorted her out of the building. "I need to practice driving here so you don't have to do all the work. I'm afraid I'll accidentally pull out onto the wrong side of the road or hit the windscreen wipers instead of the blinker."

"I can help you," she said with a laugh. "My father was a driving instructor, and I picked up a few things from him."

"Nice! Our dates will be dinner and driving. Not exactly my idea of fun but…"

"Oh, it should be fun," Lisa Marie purred. "At least what comes after will be. It will make up for any boredom the driving sessions cause you."

Devin swallowed hard. He remembered her idea of fun from the night before. She may have been seventeen years older than him, but that woman had the stamina of someone his age. "Well then…"

*****

Loralin parked her car as far away from the Roadway Hotel's office as she could. She didn't want to take up the parking space for potential customers. With the gift basket in hand, she walked along the sidewalk until she was outside the office and paused. There was a chance that Butch might chew her out, but she was grateful that he'd taken the patrons that she couldn't.

When she entered, the bell above the door rang, and within seconds, Butch stuck his head out of the back office. "Hello, Butch."

"To what do I owe the honor, Loralin?" The smile on the man's face didn't seem to correspond with the chewing out she'd somewhat expected.

"I just wanted to bring you this small token of our appreciation for helping us out when we were forced to close." Loralin noticed that the smile on Butch's face had been replaced by a look of concern. He was staring out the window.

"What on earth?" he said.

Loralin turned to look in the direction of his discomfort. A group of policemen surrounded her ex-husband as they walked up to the door. "This doesn't look good," she murmured.

The bell rang, and Miles stepped inside with his gang of men. "I'm sorry to have to do this, Butch, but you're under arrest for the murder of Penny Carlisle…"

Loralin didn't hear what else was said as the men cuffed Butch and took him from the building. She was too busy searching for her phone in her bag. The damn thing wasn't there; she must have left it in the car. "Butch, where are your keys? I'll lock up for you."

"On the wall in the office. Sara McGuire's phone number is on my desk. Please call her and ask her to come in as soon as she can." The old man looked scared, and it broke Loralin's heart. She couldn't help but feel that she had just caused an innocent man to be arrested.

"Miles, can I speak to you for a moment?" she said with clenched teeth. "What the hell are you doing arresting him?"

"Really, Loralin?" She had always hated that incredulous tone of his. "You're the one who gave him to me as a suspect!"

"Yes, Miles. A suspect to be investigated, not arrested. What evidence do you even have?"

Miles sighed and turned away from his ex to give instructions to the other officers. He then turned back to her. "So now, just a few hours after you called me begging me to consider him as a suspect, you no longer believe he's guilty?"

"Well," she said in a singsong voice. "I just didn't think you could investigate it that quickly. I mean, what kind of evidence showed up that suddenly?"

Miles looked at her like she was the biggest pain in his ass, but then his expression softened just a bit. "All I can tell you is that he doesn't have a verifiable alibi, his fingerprints were found on the back door of the inn and the kitchen door. He had a motive, and about twenty people heard him threaten her."

"Oh, come on, Miles!" she insisted. "More than a dozen people had fingerprints on those doors. The place was a madhouse on opening day."

Miles was getting frustrated with her again. "I've made a good arrest, Loralin. You've never questioned me before, so why start now? If you think he didn't do it, prove it, and I'll set him free."

"He didn't do it, Miles. I don't know how I know that, but I do. Your instinct used to be spot on, just like mine. It just isn't what it used to be anymore."

*****

Once Sara McGuire had shown up, Loralin left the motel in

her capable hands and headed to her car. She had to find a way to fix this. The guilt was crushing her, and all she could do was think of how badly she needed Devin at that moment. But he was on a date, and he might think she was trying to sabotage it if she called.

Her phone was picked up and put back down half a dozen times as she drove back to the inn. Once she was locked safely inside her house, she knew she had to make a final decision on whether to call Devin. He was the only one she could share this with. But would it wait until after his date? Could it wait until morning if that is when she next saw him? Would she even be able to sleep if she didn't talk it through with him?

Deciding there was no one else she could think of to call, she picked up her phone and dialed his number. She would make it up to him somehow. "Devin, I need you."

"Loralin? What happened? Is everything okay at the inn?" At least she was only interrupting his dinner and not something more personal. The background noise told her he was someplace very public.

"The inn is fine, but I need to talk to you. I think I've made a terrible mistake." Loralin's voice was shaky, but no tears had threatened yet. "They've arrested Butch Matthews for the murder, and I really don't think he did it."

"But I thought he was our prime suspect." Loralin heard him whisper something to Lisa Marie.

"I know. He was so good for it. But something just doesn't feel right, and I never thought Miles would make an arrest so quickly."

"Damn, I'm sorry, Loralin. What do we do now?" She hoped she hadn't ruined this whole experience for Devin. She cared about him too much. The hope had been that it would be the first 'in-person' thing they could bond over.

"We have to prove he's innocent. I guess we'll talk about it soon. Like when you get home?" She sure hoped he hadn't planned to stay the night with the pretty housekeeper. She needed him right now.

"Come get me, Loralin. I'm at Elk River Chinese Buffett."

"I owe you one, Devin. Thanks."

*****

"I'm sorry, Lisa Marie. I've got to cut our date short." He felt bad, but at this point, Loralin needed him, and that was the most important thing.

"She needs you, and you just go running? Is she sick or hurt?" He thought Lisa Marie looked a bit troubled, but he wasn't quite good at reading her yet.

"Yeah. It's how we are. I don't expect you to understand, but that's the way it is." Nobody ever understood, so why should he expect her to?

Lisa Marie looked wary. "Are you sure you two aren't together? I mean, sometimes it seems like you are."

"I promise you, we're not. It's like this super intense relationship except without sex, desire, or romantic love. I'm sorry, that's the best I can explain it." Devin set three twenty-dollar bills on the table and stood. "Text me and let me know if you want to go out again. I really hope you do. I like you a lot."

He really did like her. He could see a long-term fling with her if not a future. But in his world, Loralin was more important right then. It wasn't long before the dark SUV pulled to the curb in front of him, and he walked around the vehicle to settle into the passenger side.

Loralin didn't say much on the ride back to the inn. It wasn't until they were locked inside her office that they started to strategize. "I wish I could explain this feeling I'm having better. It's like once I told Miles, I started having second thoughts. Even the evidence against him seems off in some way."

"Do you think they could make a case that would result in a conviction?" Devin read over the notes that she'd made in her notebook about the evidence they had.

"I don't know," she said with a loud sigh. "I guess it depends on which side has the better lawyer."

Devin trusted her instincts. She was very rarely wrong about things like this. But how did they prove that Butch Matthews was innocent? "What evidence could free him? Or do we have to prove that someone else did it to get him out of this mess?"

"I just don't know." She sounded like she was about to burst into tears. "Let's take this step by step and look at the evidence they have against him. We need to get the information straight from him, though."

"Okay." Devin took a notebook from her supply closet and grabbed a pen out of the holder on the desk. "Do you think they'll let us visit the prisoner?"

"I'm sure I could convince the person in charge. The guys down at the station have always liked me."

*****

A quick stop at the house had allowed Loralin to change clothes and doll up a bit. By the time she walked into the station, she was hotter than Devin had ever seen her. He wasn't used to make-up, cleavage, or high heels. She didn't do too badly for an old lady.

"Well, hello there, Logan."

The young man looked up and smiled. "Howdy, Miss Loralin. Are you here to see Detective Robbins?"

Loralin got a kick out of how his eyes moved quickly, back and forth from her face to her chest. "Actually, I'm not. Have you guys transferred Butch Matthews to Boone yet?"

"No ma'am. Boone is full up until tomorrow. He'll be spending the night here." Logan still had his little eye problem, and both Devin and Loralin were trying not to laugh.

"Well, darlin', do you think I could visit him real quick? He was pulled out of the Roadway so fast that I had to close up for him. I'd like to let him know that everything is okay and being looked after." Logan seemed so enthralled with her large bosom that she probably could have just shaken them, and he would have said yes.

"Well, visiting hours are almost over… but I guess I could make an exception. The poor man hasn't stopped crying since he got here. He could probably use a friend." He pulled keys off the wall and exited the booth where he sat. "Follow me. You'll only have about twenty minutes."

Loralin and Devin both knew that would be plenty of time.

*****

"My hotel?" Butch asked as he was led into the room.

"It's fine. Your people are handling everything." Loralin thought the man looked like he'd aged twenty years in just a short few hours. "Look, Butch, we've known each other a long time, and I don't believe you did this. If you tell us your story, we will do everything we can to get you out of here."

The old innkeeper looked at Loralin and then at Devin. "Who's he?"

"Hello, sir. It's nice to meet you. I'm Devin Wentworth. I'm Loralin's best friend."

The room was eerily quiet for a bit too long. "Is he trustworthy?" the old man asked.

"Yes, sir. Now, can you tell us about your movements that day?" Loralin was remembering when the old man had worked for her grandfather in what was now the Robbins' Nest. He hadn't always been so grumpy and quick to fire off bad words. That all happened after his wife left him.

Well, I woke up and took the dog for a walk. Then I drove into the hotel and checked on everything, biding my time until you opened your doors. I just had to see what you'd done with the place."

"I know you had lunch and dinner with us. I appreciate your patronage."

The man just nodded and looked off into space. "I walked around, toured the place, had some lunch, took lots of notes to see what I could do to refurbish the Roadway so she would be more sellable, then I went to talk to my old friend Peter…"

"Wait, you went to talk to Chef Pierre?" she interrupted him. "Did you go into the kitchen to talk to him, perhaps?"

"Of course," the old man said as if she already should have known the information. "You know the chef rarely comes out of his cave until the end of the night."

Loralin knew that to be true. And now she knew why his fingerprints had been on the doors leading to the kitchen. "Did you also go out back?"

"Why yes, I did. I went out there to smoke. I didn't want to clog up your entrance on opening day."

Loralin and Devin were both getting excited, but they still didn't have enough to free him. "Okay, go on." Devin encouraged.

"Well," he said with a shrug. "After I saw Peter, I headed out to smoke, and I ran into Deke Robertson, you know, the man who owns those fancy hotels in Casper?"

Loralin knew the man all too well. He was a snake in the grass who had tried to trick her grandparents out of their property. "Wait a minute, you said you wanted to make the Roadway more sellable? Were you thinking of selling to Deke?"

"I hadn't until I saw him there. I approached him, and we had dinner together to discuss the possibilities."

Devin shifted in his seat. "Is there any proof that you were trying to sell? Did you and Deke agree on anything?"

The old man suddenly looked defeated. "No. Deke was going to contact me when he was back in town from his vacation in Cabo or some such place. I mean, I asked around a bit, and I know Chloe knew. Her mom and I are seeing each other, and it just came out at dinner one night."

Now, Loralin was confused. "Wait a second. If you were going to sell, then why were you so upset with Penny for leaving?"

A blush colored the old man's face. "I think I was actually mad at you, Loralin. You know, your grandfather and I had such a rivalry that he always won. And then the inn shut down, and I was a big man in the industry." He chuckled and looked sweetly at Loralin. "Then along came this little spitfire woman, taking my best workers. I just kinda lost it, and Penny was the bearer of the bad news, so to speak. I don't even know where the threat part came from. I'd never hurt anyone. Everyone in this town knows I'm all bark and no bite. Including that no good ex-husband of yours."

The trio remained quiet for a bit, then Devin broke the silence. "So, what happened after you met with Deke?"

"Well," the old man said. "Deke left, and I stayed for dessert. I went out back one last time to smoke, then drove back to the hotel for the overnight shift. And no, it isn't weird that I had the smoke first. I don't allow it in my car or inside the hotel."

"Did anyone see you?" Devin already knew the answer since he didn't have an alibi.

"Not that I know of. I sat behind the desk for about an hour watching television, and then I fell asleep. If anyone came in, they didn't bother me."

Devin and Loralin stood up to leave and let the old man get back to his cell. But just as they were walking out, she thought of something. "Butch, did you go anywhere other than the first floor?

"No, why?" He was puzzled by her question.

"What kind of gloves do your housekeepers use?"

"Those purple ones or blue, whatever color that is. The ones without powder because I'm allergic." He was looking back and forth between the best friends.

"Do you have any proof of your allergy?" Devin knew exactly where Loralin was headed with this. He just hoped they could convince Miles.

"I was rushed to the hospital in Boone about fifteen years ago when we first discovered it. Gloves didn't used to have no fancy powder shit. It was the first time I had used some."

Loralin turned to the old man and pulled him into a quick hug. "Sleep well tonight. I'm sure everything is going to be okay."

*****

Loralin and Devin headed toward the front door and stopped to thank Logan, who blushed slightly when he looked at her chest. His face suddenly fell, and the pair turned to where he was looking.

"Loralin, what's this I hear about you talking to my prisoner?"

"Seriously, Miles, give it up. The poor man is scared to death, and I'm the only one who knows what happened at the hotel after you dragged him out of there."

Miles didn't seem to appreciate the way he was being talked to. "You're the one who led us to him. So until you have information to the contrary, stay out of it."

"I do have information, Miles dear. But I need to look through it before I give it to you. "I'll be here at eight in the morning." She turned around, grabbed Devin's hand, and walked out.

They were quiet until they reached her SUV. "Why didn't we just tell him what we knew right then? Why wait until tomorrow?"

"Because Miles is always a grumpy ass after seven p.m. Besides, it will be quicker for me to gather some of the information than for the Elk River police department to do it. I love the guys, don't get me wrong, but they move at a snail's pace. They wouldn't survive one day in a big city police department."

Devin knew what it was like growing up in a small town with a lackluster police department. He trusted Loralin implicitly in this case. But he knew they were nowhere close to being done with this tonight. "How about we stop and get some snacks and drinks? I think it's gonna be a late night."

13

Suspects & More Suspects

By two a.m., they had found out that Deke was indeed in Cabo and was due home in a week. They, however, hadn't been able to get a hold of him, so Miles and his crew would have to do it. They were also able to find out that yes, the hospital in Boone did keep records from fifteen years before, but it would take a while to find them, and again, Miles would have to do that through proper channels.

"Wait a sec," Devin said as he and Loralin prepared to head to sleep. "When did we find out for sure that the powder residue from the knife was the stuff they put in the gloves?

"Don calls me every day and tells me what they have or haven't found out yet. You were asleep the other night when he called."

They decided together that Loralin would see Miles in the morning and then head over to the Roadway to see if she could scare up a witness to Butch's nap at the hotel the night of the murder. Devin had been assigned to see if he could talk to Mr. Graves. He was still the other possible AU and hadn't been ruled out yet.

*****

Luckily for Devin, Mr. Augustine Graves took a walk every morning at about 9 a.m. out by the pond. Today, he decided he would join him. "Good morning, Mr. Graves."

"Well, good morning, young man. How are you on this beautiful sunny day?" The old man seemed extra chipper. Maybe he was relieved that Penny was gone and couldn't ruin his marriage.

"I'm fine, sir. I hear you used to live here in Elk River."

"Ah, yes. This is one of my favorite places on earth. It's just hard to live here when the cold messes up my old joints." The old man sat on a nearby bench and motioned for Devin to join him.

"At least you get to come back and visit," Devin said quietly. "That must be nice. Does your family still live here?"

"I have two daughters in Casper and a son here in Elk River." The old man seemed distracted. Devin didn't think he was going to get an old timer's stories out of this conversation anymore. "Can I ask you a question, son?"

"Of course," Devin answered kindly. What was with the personality change in the old man?

"I know you hang out with Loralin. And I know her husband is the lead detective on Penny's case. Would you happen to know if they still suspect me?"

Devin was relieved he didn't have to bring up the information in the conversation. "I wasn't sure if they did or not." He didn't want to come right out and give him all the information they had. He didn't want to be the one who let a killer get away.

"Oh, come on now," Mr. Graves said with a hearty laugh. "The first two letters of my name were possibly being written in blood on my car. And then there's…"

Devin waited a few moments to see if the old man would continue on his own. "And then there's what?" he finally prompted.

"You have to know by now, the whole town knows, I think. Penny was my mistress about ten years ago. And as far as I know, my wife never knew a thing about it. And that right there is my motive."

"Well, yeah, I heard about it. But I don't know what, if anything, the police have done to investigate it. They seem kinda slow around here."

Augustine laughed. "You can say that again. Always have been and always will be. The thing is, son, that my wife actually did know from the beginning. During our first few hours here, she confessed it to me. I had no reason to kill that poor girl."

Devin was shocked. "Shouldn't you tell Detective Robbins that? It will get you off the hook." Why on earth hadn't he gone to the police yet?

"Well, if they didn't know about it, I didn't want to stir it up." He looked down at his old, wrinkled hands and shrugged his shoulders. "I guess I was scared and wasn't thinking."

"Well, I can tell you that they know about you and Penny, and they don't think your wife knows. You need to go see the detective as soon as possible to get ruled out."

The old man smiled and stood. "Thanks, young man. I feel much better now."

"You're welcome, sir." This had been much easier than he'd thought. For all he knew, he could have confronted the old man and gotten yelled at. And he would have been badmouthed through the whole town. At least that's how it happened in a lot of the books that Loralin kept around the house. Hopefully, she was having the same kind of luck.

*****

It was lunchtime when Loralin finally made it back to the Robbins' Nest. Devin was on the phone with the vending machine company, letting them know that one of the machines on the third floor was not working properly. When he hung up, his boss motioned for him to join her in the office.

"So, how did it go?" he asked as he made himself comfortable in the chair across from her desk.

"Good. I think Miles was low-key happy to hear that we might be able to clear Butch. It's really hard for him to admit that I was right, though, but he's always been that way." Loralin looked peaceful but tired.

"Maybe you should go home early and get some sleep. You know, old women get tired quicker." He knew the teasing would cheer her up. And it did.

"You are such a brat!" she said, swatting at him. "One of these days, I'm going to smack you silly for calling me old. Now tell me what happened with Augustine Graves."

Devin went right into his story. "He approached the subject first. He was afraid to tell the police that his wife had known all along about his affair with Penny. If they didn't know about the affair, he didn't want to bring it up."

"Oh, that poor man. I hope he will come clean with Miles. I think the department was planning on questioning him again, specifically about the affair with Penny. Apparently, he had lied about it the first time."

"Well then," Devin said with a yawn. Loralin wasn't the only one who was tired. "Where does that leave us now? We have absolutely no suspects anymore. And once they clear Butch... I don't know where to look now."

"Come on, let's go grab lunch. I guess we get on with life

until something jumps out at us." She felt helpless and hopeless. Maybe this case would never be solved, and her inn would always have that stigma. Even if it brought in people, there were still so many possible guests that it could scare off.

*****

Lunch was spent in the dining room with the guests and people from town. Chef Pierre's meals were becoming well talked about, and Devin and Loralin were discussing names for the eatery. They might as well make it a regular destination for not only inn guests but for anyone who wanted a good meal.

"I guess we can give this list to Chef Pierre," Devin said between bites. "We can see which one he likes best and go from there."

Loralin agreed, then sat back in her seat. She was contemplating heading home when one of the desk clerks rushed in with a message that there was an angry man at the front desk. "I'll be right there, Cody. And after this, I'm cutting out early. I'll see you at home."

Devin wasn't about to let her face an angry man alone, so he followed her up to the front. A blond man with fire in his eyes stood at the counter yelling about needing to talk to Loralin right away.

"Jace. What on earth is wrong?" she asked the man.

"Loralin. Oh, thank goodness. I need to get Penny's stuff."

"Come into my office, and we can talk privately," she invited. She motioned for Devin to come along, too. "Devin, this is Jace Carlisle, Penny's current husband."

"I'm so sorry for your loss," he said, reaching out to shake the other man's hand. "I'm afraid the police took everything of Penny's. You'll have to speak to them about getting it back."

The man looked like he was about ready to collapse, so Devin helped him into a chair. "Thank you. I'm sorry about creating a scene, but this whole thing has been a nightmare. "I was away camping when it happened. I've had a hell of a time getting back home, and I just want to rest and mourn."

Loralin offered him a bottle of water and then sat in her chair. "If there is anything we can do for you, don't hesitate to ask. I always had a soft spot in my heart for Penny."

Jace sat forward in the chair, looking a bit better. "Do you know of a good lawyer? They want me to prove that I was camping and not here killing Penny. I can't do that."

"They always suspect the husband," Devin said. "But you two had a good marriage, right? At least that's what I've been hearing."

"Well, we do for the most part, but we had a huge fight right before I went camping, and we had a few witnesses." He looked a bit peaked again, but was holding up overall.

"I would go for Mark Simpson out of Douglas," Loralin said, tearing a piece of paper off her notebook and writing a number on it. "He is the best criminal lawyer in the state."

Jace thanked them, stood carefully, and made his way to the door. "Thanks again, Loralin."

Once he was gone, she got that look, the one that said her mind was working overtime. "I think we should look into Jace. He's always been a stand-up guy, but I also hear he can have quite a temper when he's drunk."

"After you go home and rest. I'll finish up here and meet you there. We'll put a couple of steaks on the barbecue, and then we can discuss our new potential suspect.

*****

Loralin was in the kitchen making a salad when Devin walked in the back door. "Hey, how are things at the Inn?"

"Running smoothly," he said, dropping a kiss on her cheek. "It's so nice coming home to a smile and not a verbal beating for something I may or may not have done."

"I mean, if you'd rather, I can chew your ass out for something," she teased.

Devin chuckled and moved to the refrigerator. "Nah, I'm good."

"Get those going," she suggested. "The potatoes are almost done, and this salad is about to go back into the fridge until dinner. And then we try to find out if Jace is a murderer or not."

While the steaks were cooking, Devin was going over things in his mind. He'd asked around the inn while he finished up work. It seemed that not many people knew Jace very well. He wasn't originally from Elk River. And how on earth could they find out if he'd actually been camping? These would be things he would have to ask Loralin.

"Those steaks ready?" she called out the patio door.

"Yep! Coming right up."

Loralin's stomach growled as she and Devin filled their plates. Once they were done, she made the first move to talk about Jace. "So, I called Miles to see what he knew about Jace, and they don't have much more than we do. He moved here ten years ago or so. He's worked at the power company the whole time, has no criminal history, and seems very unlikely to have committed murder. But he has no alibi that has been corroborated yet."

"How well do you know him?" Devin asked between bites.

"Not really well," she admitted. "Just from around town. And of course, I've witnessed a couple of his drunken rants. He's known for putting dents in his truck by hitting it when he's fighting with Penny."

"Do you think he could ever have turned that on her?" he asked. "Has he ever been seen hitting anything other than his truck?"

"Not that I know of," Loralin said, tipping the bottle of salad dressing over her bowl. "Normally, I wouldn't think of him as a potential murderer, but he was acting strange today. He's either a drama queen when he's sober, or he was acting like he was overwhelmed and devastated."

Devin could see her point. He'd had the words drama queen run through his mind, too. "Is there anyone we could ask?"

Loralin thought for a moment. "Penny was probably the only one who would have known. His friends are all from out of town and come here once or twice a year to visit and go hunting or camping."

"That comes to my next question," Devin said, helping himself to another baked potato. "Was it like him to go camping alone this time of year?"

"Now that I know the answer to," she said, "He goes camping a lot in the spring. So yes, it could be completely normal to have gone this time. And according to Miles, a ranger saw him a few times over the week, so he just has to find him."

"Which means," Devin admitted with a sigh. "We really have nothing to investigate."

"Exactly. Besides, I don't recall ever seeing him at the grand opening. All we can do is keep our eyes and ears open, and if you think of something to ask someone, just do it." Loralin looked depressed and anxious. She wanted this person caught.

"Hey, if it isn't him, we'll find out who. It just might not be as quickly as you want."

Loralin nodded her agreement, but she didn't look happy

about it.

14

Kiss and Make Up

The day Loralin dreaded had arrived. That night, she would be having dinner with Don Peterson, and then she would be sitting next to him at the Chase Goldman concert. To save herself some distress, she would be driving to Casper to meet Don. He'd offered to come to Elk River and pick her up, but at least this way she would have an escape plan. "I bribed Don with this date, and it got us nowhere. Getting the crime scene people up here faster did nothing to help the case."

Devin felt bad for his best friend, but there wasn't much he could do about it at that point. "You never know, some of the evidence they gathered might come in useful when they get a viable suspect."

"Yeah, true. I guess this won't be so bad. I'm having a steak dinner and getting to see a concert I've wanted to see for a while now." It had been almost a week since they had discussed Jace as a suspect, and he'd since been cleared. So now would be a good opportunity to see if Don had any ideas.

"Now that's the spirit! You'll be having a great time on your date, and I'll be having a great time on mine." Devin and Lisa Marie had been seeing each other almost every night. He could tell it still bothered Loralin a little bit, but she never said anything.

"I think I'd rather go out with Lisa Marie," she mumbled as she grabbed her keys off the desk. "I guess I should get going. If you're late to Monroe's Steak House, they cancel your reservation."

Devin pulled her into a hug. "Drive safe, and I'll see you when you get home."

*****

The thirty-minute drive between Elk River and Casper was nothing for Loralin. She'd done it so many times she could probably have done it in her sleep if need be. The only problem was that the road could get a bit boring, and she was feeling drained. Her windows were rolled down, and her music was blasting to make the time go faster and to keep her mind on something besides who she was having dinner with.

The interstate was unusually quiet for this time on a Saturday evening, which made the drive even more boring than normal. There was nothing to keep her alert and on her toes. She always hated it when her mind wandered while she was driving. At least the motor home in front of her would keep her concentrating for a while. It was going so slowly, and they were in a no-passing zone.

"Don't slow down anymore, man. I want to get to Casper tonight, not tomorrow," she murmured to the vehicle in front of her. It seemed the motorhome wasn't listening, and she had to slam on her brakes when it suddenly did the same. Her car wasn't slowing down, though, so she pumped the brakes, and still nothing. Her eyes moved from side to side to see what her options were. To the left was open road, and coming up on the right was the turnoff for a ranch. It would be safer to engage her emergency brake on the dirt road, so she swerved to the right and held on tight as the car bounced through pothole after pothole. She felt stable enough to engage the brake, but when it didn't work, panic set in. Was it just her luck that her regular brakes and her emergency brakes failed at the same time?

The main thing about the bumpy dirt road is that it had slowed her down. Now she had to find a place to crash land as softly as possible. Her choices were a dirt bank and an old out-of-commission telephone pole. She chose the dirt bank, hoping it was softer than the pole. She felt the bump of her tires hitting the dirt and prayed that she wouldn't roll the car. And then her world faded to black.

"Where the hell am I?" she murmured, her eyes coming open. "This can't be good."

*****

Devin was being taught to drive American-style by Lisa Marie on the outskirts of town. The old deserted farmland was where many teens learned to drive every day. "So, how am I doing?" he asked from the driver's seat of Lisa Marie's SUV.

"Amazing. You'll be confident enough to get your license in no time."

"Good," he said, getting out of the vehicle and trading places with the actual licensed driver. "I'm getting tired of having to bum a ride off of everyone. I want my own car so I can go where I want to, when I want to."

"It will be nice for you," Lisa Marie agreed. "So, what do you want to do now that your driving practice is over?"

Devin's phone rang with the number of the inn. "This is

Devin."

"Devin, this is Maureen. A Captain Don Peterson has been trying to get a hold of you for the last hour or so. Would you like me to give him your cell number?"

Devin suddenly felt like his heart was going to beat out of his chest. Why was Loralin's date calling him? "Yes. Please give it to him."

"Is everything okay?" Lisa Marie asked when he hung up the phone.

"I'm not sure. Loralin's date has been trying to reach me for the last hour. I can't imagine why." As soon as he stopped speaking, the phone rang again, and he answered on speakerphone. "This is Devin."

"Devin, this is Loralin's friend Don Peterson. Chief of police in Cheyenne."

"Yes, Don, how can I help you?"

"Well, have you seen Loralin? We were supposed to have a date tonight, and she never showed up for dinner. Have you seen her?"

"Well, last I saw her, she was headed to Casper to meet you. Have you tried calling her?"

"Yes, and it just goes to voicemail. My buddies and I from the sheriff's department and the highway patrol are going to head toward Elk River. Is there any way you could head toward Casper? If we are both looking from different directions, we'd have a better chance of finding her if she's on the road."

Devin looked at Lisa Marie, and the woman nodded that she would be happy to drive him. "We'll head out right now."

"Thank you, young man," Don said. "We'll meet you somewhere along the way."

Devin was downright petrified. He couldn't fathom coming

all this way just to lose Loralin now. As the miles passed by and the sky got darker and darker, his anxiety grew. "Where on earth could she be if she wasn't on the side of the road somewhere? The scary possibilities threatened to take over his mind, but he couldn't let them. He had to find Loralin.

"Hey, what's that up there?" Lisa Marie said, pointing to some lights off to the side of the road ahead. "Are those police lights?"

Devin figured that was probably Don and his buddies. "Yes, I think it is. Let's pull over there and see what's going on.

"You got it." Lisa Marie turned down the ranch access road and came up behind two police cars and Loralin's SUV. She hadn't even stopped the car when Devin wrenched his door open and jumped out.

"Is she okay?" he asked, heading straight for Don. "Where is she?"

"She's not here, son," he said, putting a calming hand on Devin's arm. Her phone was smashed in the crash, so she left it here. She either walked or got a ride from somebody. We are checking the ranch at the end of this road and the hospitals in Casper and Boone."

None of this information helped Devin feel any better. He just wanted to see her, to see she was alright. "So, what now? Do we just wait here?"

"We're hoping to hear something soon so we know which direction to head," Don said.

"Devin!" Lisa Marie stepped out of her vehicle and ran up to him. "Your phone."

It was ringing when he took it, and he answered. "This is Devin."

"Devin, my name is Miranda. I'm a nurse at Wyoming

Medical Center in Casper. Loralin asked me to call you for her. Are you able to speak to her now?"

"Yes!" put her on." Now all of the cops were gathered around him listening, so he once again hit speakerphone.

"Hey, Dev." She sounded scared.

"Hey. What happened? Are you okay?"

"Uh, yeah, I'm okay, just in shock. Could you call Miles and have him come up here? And you come with him, please. I need to see you."

"I'm already halfway to Casper. We're at the crash site. "I'll find a way to get there."

"Okay, Dev. Love you."

"Love you too, Loralin."

"We'll give you a lift back to Casper," Don said. And it was a good thing because when Devin looked back at where Lisa Marie had been parked, he saw her SUV turning back onto the highway. He'd have a lot of explaining to do the next day.

*****

Loralin was sitting propped up in the ER bed when Devin walked in. "Hey, are you okay? Where are you hurt?"

She smiled at him as tears came into her eyes. "Give me a hug first."

Devin took her into his arms and held on for dear life. They'd never thought they would be able to meet, and now they had. There was no way they could lose each other now. "So, you want to tell me what's going on?"

"You know that bad luck I have on occasion?"

"Yes," he answered warily. "What about it?"

"Well, my brakes went out and so did my emergency brake." She shrugged and smiled at him, "I had to run the car onto a dirt road and into a dirt pile to get it to stop."

"Did you hit your head? How did you get here?" He was so full of questions, but he wanted to make sure she was okay first.

"No, I didn't hit my head, but I did pass out," she admitted. "I guess I was in shock when the Marshall family from Elk River came along and gave me a ride to the hospital. I really don't remember much about the ride into town."

"And you've been checked over by the doctor?" he asked. "What did they say?"

"Excuse me," came the voice of an older man in a white doctor's coat. "How are you feeling, Loralin?"

"Stronger by the minute, Doc.," she said with a smile. "This is my best friend, Devin. Devin, this is Doctor Winger."

"Nice to meet you," Devin said. "How is she?"

"Don't worry, young man. She is fine. No injuries, just a bit of shock. I want her to rest for a couple of days, and she'll be good as new."

Devin almost felt like crying with the relief he felt. It would take more than this to keep them apart. "That's great. Thank you, doctor."

Once the older man had left, Devin sat down in a chair next to the bed and grabbed her hand. "I guess that means they will release you soon."

"Yeah," she said softly. She was obviously exhausted. "Did you call Miles?"

"Yes. He's on his way. He will be our ride home."

"Okay. Now I just have to arrange to have my car towed home so I can get it looked at by my Mechanic." She didn't sound happy about having to do it. She sounded like she just wanted to sleep for a few days.

"It's all taken care of," Devin told her as her eyes drooped.

"Don might be a little creepy, but he sure takes care of the people he likes. "Your car will be in McGee's shop before we get home."

Loralin pulled herself out of sleep. "Shit. And I must apologize to Don."

"Don't worry about that now," he said in soothing tones. "He's fine now that he knows you're okay. Why don't you try to get some sleep, and I'll go see when we can get you out of here."

*****

It was nearly two a.m. before Loralin was checked out, and they piled into Miles's car to head back to Elk River. "How are you feeling now?" Devin asked.

"Better," Loralin answered. "And I'm starting to wonder if it's time for a new car."

Miles, who had been quiet since he'd arrived at the hospital, turned to his ex-wife. "It won't be necessary. It wasn't the car's fault.

"What do you mean?" both Loralin and Devin asked before Miles could finish his thought.

"I mean, the brake lines were cut, and the emergency brake was tampered with."

Loralin was quiet for so long that Devin worried she'd gone into shock again. "Are you saying that someone tried to kill her?"

"That's what I'm saying," Miles said in his most serious tone. "What in the hell have you been doing at that inn? It seems you investigated the wrong person."

"But that's the whole thing, Miles," she finally said. "We haven't investigated anyone. We used information about the case to find likely people, but things ruled them out before we even really had to interrogate anyone."

"She's right, Miles," Devin defended. "We haven't made anybody uncomfortable. If you asked around the hotel, no one would guess that we'd been investigating the murder on the side."

Miles was tensed up but trying to relax so he could drive properly. "Well then, why did someone try to kill you?"

"I don't know," Loralin admitted. "But I'm going to find out."

"Loralin!" Miles warned. But he knew better than to get on her case too much because when she was determined, nothing, including death, would stop her.

"The question is, is this related to Penny's murder or is it something completely different?" Devin's thought was on everyone's minds as they sat quietly for the rest of the trip back to Elk River.

*****

"Any news?" Devin asked as he joined Loralin in her office at the inn. She'd rested up for two days, and then he'd encouraged her to go back to work.

"No, nothing yet. Miles is still investigating anyone who might have been angry that I helped him put them away. So far, he hasn't found anything."

"What about people who might be angry that you reopened the inn?" he asked. "Did you or your grandparents have any enemies?"

"Nothing that stands out. We know Butch did but that was years ago and he doesn't seem mad at me anymore."

"Something is nagging at the back of my mind. I'm just not sure exactly what it is." It was so frustrating for Devin because he knew that if he could straighten out the feeling, he might be able to help solve the mysteries.

Devin was just about to leave to grab them some lunch from the dining room when Chloe walked in. "Hey guys, there is something stuck under the cabinet in the supply room. The broom handles won't quite reach it. Got any ideas?"

"What's under there?" Loralin asked. "And how did it get there?"

"It looks like an open box of our gloves," Chloe said with a shrug. "I noticed there was one missing off the cart when I came in the morning, Penny died. I thought maybe she'd put it somewhere else. But when I dropped my master keys this morning, they went just under the edge of the cabinet, and I saw the box."

Devin turned to the housekeeper. "You noticed one missing and didn't report it?"

"I was going to tell Penny, and then, well, you know. With all the chaos, I kind of forgot."

Loralin stood and headed out of the office. "Devin, call Miles and tell him to come here and meet us in the supply room."

Apparently, Loralin had the same train of thought that Devin had. "He pulled his phone out of his pocket and dialed.

*****

Miles and two other officers walked in the front doors of the inn to find Devin waiting for them. "What's going on?"

"One of the housekeepers found an open box of gloves under the cabinet in the supply room. They had first noticed it was gone the day of the murder, but with all the chaos, it never got reported."

"And we know our killer used gloves," Miles said as they made their way up to the supply room. "I'm also pretty sure we now know where they got them."

"That's what Loralin and I were thinking," Devin admitted.

When they arrived at the supply room, Loralin and Chloe were there with a wooden pole from goodness knew where. "Would you like to do the honors, Detective?"

"You know it, Loralin. That way, any evidence isn't contaminated."

Devin found it comical that the Detective had rolled his eyes at his ex-wife. Sometimes, he thought their whole relationship revolved around challenging each other.

Chloe moved the cleaning cart out from in front of the cabinet, and Miles got down on his hands and knees with the pole in his hand. Within thirty seconds, he wriggled back, and the open box of gloves appeared on the end of the pole. One of the other officers bagged it for him while he stood up.

Miles turned to the other officer who was with him. "I need to see the results of the fingerprints from these doors," he said, pointing to the double doors that adorned the supply closet.

"There won't be any, Miles," Loralin cut in. "The doors didn't arrive until three days after the opening. We had curtains hanging in the doorway."

Miles sighed. "Well, that explains how the killer was able to get the gloves so easily. Do you know if anything else was missing from here that day?" His question was directed at both Chloe and Loralin.

"Two days after Penny died, we found that we were one short on the hotel robes," Chloe said. "We checked with guests, and none of them had it, so I'm not sure when or how it disappeared."

"Thank you," Miles said to the housekeeper. "Loralin, can I see you and Devin in your office?"

The two men followed Loralin downstairs and settled into chairs around her desk. "Is everyone else thinking what I'm thinking?" she asked.

"What?" Devin said with a smile. "That the murderer stole gloves and a robe so they wouldn't get any blood on themselves and then ditched the stuff somewhere?"

"Exactly," Miles said more seriously. "I think I need to have the woods searched again. The trash compactor was negative for blood, as was the boiler and furnace, which weren't in use yet."

Loralin sighed and rubbed her temples as if she were getting a headache. "I'll have the staff alert the guests to stay inside the building. Sometimes I think this nightmare is never going to end."

Devin was getting the same feeling. That normalcy he hoped to experience was fleeting and seemed to be getting farther away. He was determined to make sure it happened, though. The fact that the night before, his parents had told him they were ready to leave soon made him feel even better. Now all they had to do was set a date, and Loralin would buy their tickets.

*****

Devin was fielding questions at the front desk when Thomas Walden walked up to him. "Hello, Mr. Walden. Have you and your family enjoyed your vacation to Elk River?"

The man, looking as sour as ever, nodded his head. "We have. We even need to extend our stay again."

"Oh, I hope nothing is wrong." Devin and just about everyone who worked there were curious about the little family that rarely left the inn. Even the housekeepers said they only got their room cleaned twice a week, and even then, it didn't need to be cleaned a lot.

"No. Just visiting nearby family, and they need us to stay on."

"Very well," Devin said politely. "How much longer will you need the room?"

"Another two weeks, if possible," the man said, never breaking a smile. "And do you have suggestions on where to buy toys nearby?"

"Alright, Mr. Walden. You are all set for another two weeks in your current room, and my best recommendation for toys would be at the big box store in Casper, thirty miles away. I believe the nearest toy store is quite a drive down into Colorado."

The man nodded at Devin and went about his business. His wife and son joined him, and they headed to their minivan in the parking lot.

"Hey, Loralin, have you asked Miles about the Walden family? I get a weird feeling about them, but I just can't figure out what's wrong."

"All he said is that they didn't know Penny and had an alibi for when she was killed." Loralin was just as curious as he was, but right now she was preoccupied with the police scouring every inch of her property for bloody clothing.

"Do you know the family they are here to see?" he asked.

"No. I don't think so. It could be someone on the outlying ranches." She looked like she was about to lose it.

"Hey, maybe you should go home and rest. I know this has been really hard on you." She didn't look well. The stress was showing on her beautiful face.

Loralin snapped out of whatever was occupying her mind and smiled. "No, I can't leave until the police are gone. I think it makes the guests feel better that the owner is here and available. "I, however, am starving and was thinking about going to dinner. Would you like to come?"

Devin hesitated. "Umm, I was going to have dinner with my family. Would you join us?"

Loralin chuckled. "What the hell. What's a little more stress?"

They walked side by side to the dining room, where Devin's family was waiting at a round table in the corner. Loralin made sure to smile as she approached. "Good evening, everyone. I hope you've been enjoying your stay. I'm sorry I haven't been available much lately."

"We've been having a grand time," Mark said as he invited her and his son to sit. "Isn't that right, dear?"

Catherine looked at her son and smiled. "Actually, we have. I want to thank you for your hospitality, Loralin. And I want to apologize for everything I've done wrong."

"Oh, Umm..." Loralin was momentarily speechless. "Thank you, Catherine, I accept."

"Good, then maybe you'll do me a favor," Catherine said shyly. "I've been dying to go to Casper and do some shopping. Would ya like to come with me?"

Once again, Loralin was speechless. "I, well, yeah, I'd like that, Catherine. I have to go to Casper in the morning if you'd like to come along. I have to shop for some stuff for the house, and then we can hit the mall and the downtown shops if you'd like."

"It's a date then," Catherine said excitedly, clapping her hands. "I really shouldn't take my past traumas out on you. Before I met Mark, I dated an older man, and it wasn't a healthy relationship. I just worry about my kids so much. I want to save them from the painful mistakes."

For the rest of the meal, Loralin felt a little lightheaded, and she had to keep looking at Devin to see that he'd heard the same words come out of his mother's mouth. Each time he made eye contact, it told her what she needed to know. She just wondered how on earth it had happened. The story about her past almost made her seem human. It was, perhaps, a miracle in Elk River.

15

Hiding in Trees

Loralin was having so much fun with her best friend's mother. She was still in shock that their shopping trip was happening, but at least she was having a good time. She'd half expected Catherine to carjack her and leave her body in the wild somewhere between Elk River and Casper. "Where to next? Is there anything specific you wanted to check out?"

"No, I'm done spending money. Mark is gonna kill me as it is. I'm just along for the ride now." Catherine had been smiling an awful lot, and Loralin saw where Devin got his devastating smile.

Just as Loralin started the car to head to one more store, her phone rang. "Hey, Dev. What's up?"

"Loralin, you might want to get back here as soon as possible." His voice was no-nonsense.

"Oh God, what's wrong? Her heart skipped a few beats as she waited for his answer.

"One of our guests found the bloody gloves and robe," he said with a loud, harsh sigh.

"Where?" It took all of her energy at that point to say that one word.

"Mrs. Harper, who had just checked in yesterday, decided to take a walk through the woods. The wind blew the robe out of a tree right on top of her. The gloves were stuffed in the pocket."

Loralin felt like she just might die. "Is she okay?"

"Yeah, just a little shaken," he assured her. "She's a retired detective, so stuff like that doesn't bother her as much as it might have someone else."

"She'll probably sue us anyway." Loralin had lost all faith in just about everything. "Comp her stay and her meals, and we will be there in about thirty. I'm not going to kill myself speeding."

"Be safe," he said and hung up.

Loralin put her phone away and started the car. Catherine was watching her. "They found more evidence in the murder. I've got to get back."

"Oh dear," Catherine said, "I hope it helps the case. I don't think we will be here to see it resolved." Her tone had changed from the happy one she'd been using all day. It wasn't quite the mean hateful one, but it was intriguing all the same. It was like she had sensed how Loralin felt and mirrored her mood.

"Yes, Devin told me you were ready to leave." Despite the changes in tone, Loralin was kind of sad now. She'd like to get to know Catherine more. "Remind me tomorrow, when things calm down, to call and get your tickets."

"Thank ya, Loralin," Catherine said with her uncharacteristic smile. "As soon as possible, please. My auntie isn't well, and I want to go help my sisters take care of her."

There was that strange tone again. Conversation for the rest of the trip centered on Catherine and her family. It kept

Loralin's mind off the worst-case scenario that was brewing in her psyche all the time these days.

*****

Loralin had lost count of the number of times police cars had converged on her newly opened inn in the last week or two, and here they were again. Catherine headed up to her room, leaving Loralin to find Devin and Miles. The first place she checked was her office. "Ah, there you are."

"Hey," Devin said with a smile as he walked over and hugged her. "Come on, I'll introduce you. Mrs. Harper, this is Loralin Robbins, owner of the Robbins' Nest. Loralin, this is Adelle Harper."

"I am so sorry," Loralin said, shaking the woman's outstretched hand and then sitting down in a chair next to her. "I don't know how to properly apologize for this mess."

"Don't worry," the woman said with a chuckle. "I've seen worse and been attacked by worse. Besides, it's not like it's your fault. You didn't kill someone and hide evidence in that tree."

"I just wish I could have prevented it all," Loralin said, running out of steam. "This is my inn, and we've had nothing but disasters."

"Let me give you some advice," the woman said, grabbing Loralin's hand. "Mourn your employee and then run with the situation. You have an amazing marketing opportunity here. Don't mess it up."

Loralin squeezed the other woman's hand and then let it go. "Thank you for your understanding. Your room and meals will be on me during your stay."

"I thank you," the woman said, standing up. "Now that I'm done being questioned by this handsome detective, I'll be on my way back to my room. If you need anything, let me know." Mrs. Harper walked out of the room.

When Loralin finally looked over at her ex-husband, he was still blushing at the woman's comment. "So, what happens now, Miles?"

"The robe and gloves go to the state lab for analysis, and then we hope it gives us something to go on." He didn't seem as happy with the find as she thought he would be.

"I hope it doesn't take too long." She wanted this over and done with.

"They have a backlog over there because of those murders up in Jackson last month, so who knows how long it will take," he admitted. "Vic over at the lab said it could be as much as a month, depending on how fast their techs work."

Loralin wanted to tell the lab to work fast, but then would that be the best thing?" In actuality, accuracy was much more important than speed. Mrs. Harper had been right. If she put the proper spin on this, she'd be filled up for a long time to come. "Okay, so now it's back to more waiting. It's hard to go back to work and act normal with all of this hanging over our heads."

"I know," Miles sympathized. "Just do the best you can. I'll be in touch if I hear anything. And I don't believe I'm going to say this, but please keep your eyes and ears open. Several of the guests who were here during the murder are still here. Maybe they didn't realize that they saw or heard something important. Just don't get too involved in the case that you jeopardize it."

Loralin couldn't help but smile. In a roundabout way, he was giving her permission to snoop a little. "I'll do my best."

Loralin showed Miles out and came back to sit behind her desk. Devin was sitting in front of it, waiting for her. "So, what's next on the agenda? I guess it's back to work as usual once the police clear out."

"Yeah. We have the hospital in Casper that booked the dining room for their party next month. We have a hunting convention that wants to stay here in October and commute to Casper every day. We need to find a van service for them, which won't be as easy as it sounds for hunting season. Oh, and we need to hold interviews for a new head housekeeper. It's time we get someone to replace Penny, so they have more structure. I think some of the housekeepers are melting down. And, last but not least, I promised your mother I would make reservations for them to go home."

"Okay then, we have some things to work on tomorrow when it's time to come back to work. Right now, however, I am going to close out my shift and head home. And you are coming with me. I have a surprise planned for you."

Loralin had planned on working late to get some stuff done and keep her mind busy, but this was interesting enough to make her change her mind. "A surprise, huh? Wow, I can't wait to see this."

"You're going to love it," he said with a sly grin. "I'll meet you at home in half an hour."

*****

Loralin made her way up the walk leading to her house. Devin was walking out the back door and unlocking the driver's side of her rental car. A picnic basket sat by his feet. "You're taking me on a picnic?"

He looked up at her and gave her the smile she loved so much. "Yeah, but that's not the whole surprise. Climb in the passenger seat and let's go."

Every time she got in the car, she thought about the brakes

failing and almost didn't want to risk driving, even though the guard who patrolled the grounds kept an eye on her carport during the day. Plus, there were now alarms hooked up to the car that would alert someone if the car was even touched. "The passenger seat?"

"Yeah, come on." Devin's smile was proud as he got in the car and started the ignition. When she slid in next to him, he pressed the accelerator and pulled out of the carport.

"When on earth did you get so comfortable driving an American car? You always said you were a bit wary of it. And where are we going for this picnic?" She was so happy that he would have more freedom now. That had always been a concern of hers when they'd talked about him moving to be near her.

"We are going to take the old road down by the river and find a place to stop for the picnic." He was so proud of himself for conquering one of his fears. "And Lisa Marie taught me. That's been a part of all our dates in the last few days."

As they drove down the old access road that eventually led to the old mines in the hills, Loralin took a moment to enjoy the beautiful scenery and the warmth coming through the car windows. Spring in Elk River was always one of her favorite times. Everything was blooming, the river was flowing at full speed again, and the sky just seemed so much bluer than at other times of the year. Of course, soon, flooding could come when the melt-off happened in the mountains. But luckily, the inn was up on the higher ground and would be safe, even in the worst of flood seasons. "You know what? I know the perfect place. Pull over in the clearing up there, and I'll show you."

Devin did as she asked and looked around at his surroundings. Wyoming sure was beautiful. He did miss home and the green and beauty of Tasmania, but he felt content where he was now. He couldn't wait to see what a snowy winter was like. His only experience was through Loralin's eyes. There was only one thing holding him back from admitting that he was finally at home there: the issues and uncertainty of the murder were still hanging over the place. "Okay," he said, unhooking his seat belt. "Where do we go from here?"

"Do you see those two trees there? The ones that are taller than the others?" Loralin was finally looking more at ease than she'd been in days.

"Yep," he answered, getting out of the car.

"We walk between them and down a small hill. It's a place I used to play in when I was a kid." She walked around to him and grabbed the hand that didn't have the handle of the picnic basket in it. "Let's go, I haven't been down there in a couple of years."

The two friends walked side by side through the trees, and before they were even down the hill, Devin was liking what he saw. There was a clearing, relatively small in size, where trees didn't grow, and the warm sun shone down like a spotlight on the soft grass. "Wow, I can see why you like it here."

"Any time I was sad or hurt or just needed to be alone, I would come down here. And sometimes my grandmother would come looking for me, and she'd stay for an hour or two so we could just talk." Her grandmother had meant the world to her. While her mother and father had worked hard at their jobs, she'd spent most of her time with her grandmother at the inn or the cottage she now called home.

"Your grandmother sounds amazing. I wish I could have met her." Devin had also spent a lot of time with his grandparents and could sympathize with how much she missed her grandmother.

"She would have loved you," Loralin said, her voice breaking. "She loved tall, strong men who took good care of her granddaughter. She only liked Miles. She couldn't see why I'd want to marry someone who wasn't tall."

Devin chuckled. "I bet she didn't like him involving you in cases, and right now she's probably going crazy with worry up there in heaven."

Loralin laid out the blanket and sat down to start emptying the basket. "She hated the fact that Miles indulged my obsession with crime and mysteries. She even stopped buying me mystery books once I married him."

"Ah, she thought maybe if she didn't enable the dangerous hobby, you would stop." Devin poured some wine into two glasses and handed her one.

"Yep. It didn't work, though. I had my own money to buy mysteries and crime stories, so she just gave up and prayed for me."

Devin was suddenly curious. "Was she happy when you and Miles filed for divorce?"

Loralin laughed. "Probably, but she never once said so. She just held me while I cried and took the girls out for shopping and lunches and let us know she was always there for us."

"She and my grandfather would probably have gotten along. He was the type who, if you were sad or upset or having trouble at home, he'd just sit and listen and try to help you come up with a solution. But don't get me wrong, he wasn't a softie, so to speak. He was a hard ass and would spank me if I needed it. It's just that he was fairer. Punishment always fit the crime, and he never lashed out in anger."

Loralin reached over and squeezed his hand. "I wish I could

have met him."

Devin smiled sadly and handed her a plate full of food. "You guys would have gotten along so well. And not just because you're old."

Loralin cleared her throat and looked at the young man who'd just insulted her. "What did I say about calling me old?"

Devin chuckled, his sentimental melancholy gone. "You said that I could call you old anytime I wanted to."

Loralin opened her mouth in disbelief and wadded up her napkin to throw at him. "I did not."

"Are you sure about that?" Devin asked, barely able to keep a straight face. "You might just not remember. You know because you're so old."

Loralin knew when she'd been beaten. "Alright, alright, I'm old, but you love me anyway."

"I do," he said with a big grin. "You are the best friend I've ever had, and I don't know what I would do without you in my life."

"Same." Hopefully, this one picnic would keep her happy for a few days. The lack of progress and the long wait time for forensics were going to cause her so much stress. Sometimes she even prayed for a miracle so this would all be over and she could breathe freely again.

16

We Are Nowhere

A week after the picnic, Loralin found herself still handling things well. Every day progressed somewhat normally, but every time she thought about the case, especially the forensics timeline, she could feel herself getting a little anxious. They just needed a simple break to wrap it up. "Hey Devin, I found a flight for your parents, finally, that wasn't 20,000 dollars. They leave a week from today at 4:30."

"Great. I know my mum can't wait to get home to help with my Auntie." Devin seemed to be enjoying the temporary 'normalcy' that Loralin was experiencing. But he was also more than ready for a break in the case. I'm going to go see what's going on with the supplier. Three of our food orders have been late recently."

"Okay, I'll talk to you later." Loralin was walking to the bank of file cabinets behind the door when it slowly opened. A little blond head poked around the corner.

"Well, hello there," Loralin said, and Devin stopped in his tracks by the door.

"Ma'am, can I talk to you for a moment?" The little boy

looked scared out of his mind.

"Of course, you can," Loralin said as Devin ushered him to a chair. She shut the door quietly behind him. "What can I do for you? You're the Walden kid, right?"

"Yes, ma'am," he answered softly. "My name is Elliot."

"It's nice to meet you, Elliot," Loralin said. "I'm Miss Robbins, and this is my friend Mr. Wentworth."

"I know something about the lady who died. But I'm afraid to tell the police."

Loralin and Devin looked at each other and then back at the kid. "Well, you could tell us, and if we think it's important, we can stay with you while you tell Detective Robbins. Would you like that?"

"Yes, ma'am," he said softly.

"Okay, Elliot, go ahead and tell us what you know." Devin bent down in front of him. "Don't worry, you're safe here."

The little boy looked from one adult to the other. "I... Our room is right off the parking lot, and I couldn't sleep that night, so I was lying in bed reading. I... I heard noises. A woman was yelling, and then there was screaming, like someone was hurt."

"Okay, that's very good that you told someone. Can I call the detective now and have him come listen to what you have to say?"

"Yes, ma'am, I guess. But my momma and daddy are gonna be so mad."

"It's okay," Devin said. "We'll talk to your parents." He looked up at Loralin with a question in his eyes.

When she looked back at him, they both hoped the young boy would actually stay safe from his parents.

While Loralin called Miles, Devin kept the boy busy by giving him some markers and paper to draw on. He wondered if the child was more scared of talking to the police or doing something his parents would not approve of.

Loralin hung up the phone and turned to Elliot. "Hey, bud, Detective Robbins says we have to have your parents here when you talk to him, so I'm going to call up to your room and have them meet us down here, okay?"

The little boy looked terrified and stared at her for a moment. "I knew this would happen." His voice was soft and quiet. "Can you wait until the detective is here to call them?"

"Yes," Loralin said with a smile. "I think that's a good idea."

*****

Loralin stood at the window waiting for Miles's car to pull into the parking lot. When it did, she went to her desk and called the boy's parents. They were worried sick about their son and said they would be right down. "Devin, they're on their way."

Devin moved the boy over to the meeting table, where he and Loralin did all of their strategizing. He pulled over seats for the boy's parents and Miles.

Once everyone was seated, Loralin and Devin turned to leave, but little Elliot ran to them. "Please stay! Detective, mommy, daddy, please let them stay."

Miles indicated that it was okay with him, and the parents discussed things quietly and agreed.

"Hey, Elliot," Miles said once the child was seated again. "I'm Detective Robbins, and Miss Loralin told me you had something to say about the lady who died here a couple of weeks ago."

"Detective," Thomas Walden said. "I'm afraid my son is a bit bored and has wasted your valuable time. He doesn't know anything about that housekeeper."

"Yes, I do, Dad!" Elliot insisted. "I heard them yelling and screaming. I heard it."

"Son, you've been so bored lately," his mother said. "You are just making up games about the death."

"No, Mom! I really heard it." The boy sat there pouting. "I heard it, and I'm going to tell the detective no matter what you say!"

Miles looked at Elliot. "Go ahead, boy. Tell me what you heard."

"I was in bed near the window that shows the parking lot," he said, then looked at his father, who stared disapprovingly. "And I heard a lady yell, and then I heard screaming."

"And when was this?" Miles asked him.

"The time that the lady died in the parking lot." His voice faded as his mother cleared her throat. Luckily, it was still audible.

Miles wrote some notes and looked at the boy again. "Did you sit up and look out the window?"

"No, sir."

"Could you tell us if you heard the voice again?" This could be a big break in the case if he could identify the killer.

"No, sir. It was loud, and it was ladies, that's all. I couldn't hear everything she said either."

Miles made some more notes and turned to the parents. "Did either of you hear anything?"

"No. And I highly doubt Elliot did either?" Mrs. Walden said harshly.

Miles had had enough, and you could see it on his face. "Mr. and Mrs. Walden, you walk around here acting like the mob is chasing you and locking your child away in a small hotel room. And now you are trying to impede a police investigation. That actually makes you look guilty as hell, and I will arrest you for child neglect and murder if you do not stop!"

Mr. Walden's face went pale, and Mrs. Walden gasped. Loralin, always the peacemaker, came over to them. "Now, Miles, I don't think it has to come to that. Maybe the Waldens can explain what's going on, and we can help them if they are indeed in trouble."

"We can do that," Miles agreed. "If they feel comfortable enough."

"Mr. Wentworth, could you take Elliot out to the vending machine and get him a snack?" Mr. Walden said as he pulled some money out of his wallet and handed it to Devin.

Once the two were gone, Mr. Walden turned to Miles. "We were in hiding, living in Salt Lake City, and my father got sick. He, my mother, and my sisters still live in Boone. So we came home to help out and say our goodbyes, but we have to keep a low profile."

"And just who are you running from?" Miles asked. He sure hoped it wasn't the mob. That's the last thing they needed in his town.

"My son's biological mother. She's threatened to take him several times. She lives in Cheyenne, and we're terrified she will find out we're here and come get him. She's threatened all of us. We can't take the chance that we will be part of the news of this murder."

So much finally made sense to Loralin. Everything about the way they acted had an explanation, and it made her feel so much better. She wasn't harboring child abusers after all. "Can you help them, Miles?"

Miles smiled and sat back in his chair. "We will do everything we can to keep this out of the news. At this point, it has helped us identify the gender of the suspect. We can release that information without telling the public exactly how we know. If there is a time when this all must become public, we will offer you protection."

"Thank you so much, Detective," Mr. Walden said, standing and shaking his hand. "We appreciate it."

"No problem. If you need anything in the meantime, let me know." Miles turned to follow them out when he stopped. "Could you send me any information you have on your son's mother? That way, we can know what we're up against if she shows up."

"I'll do that, Detective. Thanks again."

Soon enough, Devin and Loralin were alone in the office. "So, our murderer is a woman," he said.

"Yeah. I just wonder who," Loralin questioned. "It could be any of the other housekeepers, it could be a current or former guest, hell, it could be anyone from town."

"This is so frustrating," Devin admitted. "We get new evidence, and it doesn't bring us any closer to solving the crime."

"Yeah," she said with a sigh. "If it keeps going like this, I'm going to need another picnic to make it through the month."

Devin chuckled and pulled her into a quick hug. "Yeah, me too."

*****

For the first time since Devin had arrived, Loralin was looking forward to having dinner with his family. She and Trevor had become close, and Mark seemed to really like her. Catherine had come around, and she might even consider her a friend someday.

"Loralin, is there any way ya can get us home sooner?"

Catherine asked with a hint of desperation in her voice.

"No, I'm sorry, Catherine. That's the earliest I can get unless I want to pay 20,000 dollars. I just can't afford that."

For a moment, Loralin thought the other woman was going to explode, but she didn't. She just smiled and nodded. "I understand. We'll be home before we know it."

"Yes, we will, dear," Mark said, squeezing his wife's hand. And what an adventure we can say we have had here in America."

Loralin looked over at Devin, who was in the passenger seat of her rental car. He was smiling and seemed calmer than he had the whole time he'd been there. She was pretty sure it had a lot to do with his mother and her getting along.

By the time they reached the restaurant, the subject had changed to when they might get the two over to Tasmania for a holiday visit or two. Honestly, Loralin wasn't ready for that yet, although she was sure that eventually, they would make it over there. She couldn't wait to see where Devin grew up. "I guess we'll have to see how the inn is running, what my girls are doing, and what we will be doing with respective partners."

Catherine sighed. "I keep forgetting that you two aren't a normal couple. Devin, dear, are ya still seeing that housekeeper?"

"Umm, I'm not sure, Mum. I mean, we've had a few dates recently, but she's been a little upset since the day of Loralin's accident."

"But why?" Loralin interjected.

"Well," he said, looking between his mother and his best friend. "I kinda had her drive me around to find Loralin, and then when we found her car, I kinda forgot about her and went with the police to see Loralin at the hospital."

"Oh, Devin," Loralin said. "She's already having a hard time processing our friendship."

"I know," he said apologetically. "It was a stupid mistake, but I made it, and now I'm trying to make it up to her."

"That's what I've wondered about," Catherine said softly. "Obviously, Loralin is one of the most important parts of your life, so doesn't that mean prospective girlfriends will need to understand that?"

Loralin and Devin looked at each other for a moment. "Yeah, Mum," he said. "But I just don't know how to make that happen yet?"

*****

"If you all will excuse me for a moment, I'm going to go say hi to my ex-husband." Everyone watched as Loralin walked to a table in the corner where Miles and his detective partner, Jackie, sat. "Welcome home, Jackie. It looks like you walked right into a murder."

"Yeah," she said with a smile. "I'm sure glad I had a month in the Caribbean before coming home."

"So, any news?" she said, turning her attention to Miles.

"Not really. The lab is starting to go through the ten or so footprints we were able to get around the tree where the robe and gloves were found. Other than that, we are at a loss."

"Oh, how I wish something else would turn up," Loralin said wistfully. "I need to get this solved so things at the inn can feel normal. Even if it doesn't bother potential guests, it bothers me. And I'm sure Penny's family would like some answers too."

"We all want to be done with this, Loralin," Miles said with an irritated sigh. "There just isn't that much evidence, so trying to piece what we have together is getting us nowhere; even with your help."

Loralin knew that her ex-husband was right. It was no more

his fault that they had nothing than it was hers. It was just the way things were. She excused herself and went back to the table. She pulled out her phone and texted her best friend. "After dinner, we need to sit down and list every bit of what we know about the case and see what we can come up with. There has to be a hint somewhere."

"I agree," was his reply. They risked a quick look at each other and then settled into eating their dinner.

*****

"It was nice having a stress-free dinner," Loralin said when they sat down at her dining room table with a couple of notebooks and pens.

"Stress-free for who?" Devin said. "I realized tonight that it all feels so wrong. There is no way my mother would have accepted things that quickly. But what is she up to?"

Loralin thought for a moment. "Well, maybe she just wants you to be happy when she leaves?"

"No," Devin said matter-of-factly. "She never has before, so why start now? Especially with you. She hates you."

Loralin knew he was probably right, but it all seemed genuine to her. He did know his own mother much better than anyone else, though. "Okay, let's get this list started. The first thing we know is that the killer is a woman."

"Yep," he agreed. "And the second thing we know is that the killer took a pair of gloves and a robe from the supply closet before the doors were put on… Which made it so much easier than if the door had been there and locked."

Loralin took a drink of the iced tea she'd made for herself and stared at the list she was making. It was all pretty straightforward so far. "Okay, then we know the killer took off through the woods and for some reason came to a tree where she threw the bloody clothing."

"And," Devin added. "She may or may not have left a footprint, according to what Miles told you tonight. Am I right?"

"Yeah," she said. "Then most likely, she came in the back door and went about her business. That makes me think it was someone staying here. I mean, would you go through the woods then skirt back around near the murder to get to your car and escape?"

Devin groaned and ran his fingers through his hair. "I just don't know what this person did or was thinking. The worst part is, we still don't have a motive, we don't know what the bloody markings on the car mean, and we still don't know if whoever tried to kill you is the same person and why they turned on you."

Loralin went to the cupboard and pulled down some cookies. "It's not like I was being super nosy or had my mind set on a killer."

"I know, but then that makes me wonder why you were targeted."

Loralin sat back down and took a bite of the cookie. "Well, Penny and I both had long dark hair, so it makes you think of a serial killer, but then again, nobody else here was targeted, and plenty of the staff have long dark hair."

"True," Devin agreed. "But then again, maybe she's waiting for something, or maybe she's moved on."

"So, basically what you're saying is that we are right back to where we were before… nowhere."

"Yeah," Devin said, tossing his pen down on the table. "We are nowhere."

17

Bellhops & Doctor's Notes

The next morning, Loralin had planned to take the day off, but she decided to go in long enough to talk to the nighttime bellhop. She'd been looking through the notes she'd swiped from Miles, and she'd noticed that there was a smudge right where a name was supposed to be in one part. Jeffrey, the nighttime bellhop, had given a list of people he'd seen in the inn that night, and a few of the names were too messed up to read.

Reaching out, she touched the paper where the smudge was and realized it was on her copy. Why hadn't she noticed it before? She could easily have asked Miles for the complete list. She couldn't help but feel that Miles should have placed some kind of emphasis on the people who were seen out and about in the inn at the time of the murder.

"Elk River Police Department, this is Joanne. How may I direct your call?"

"Joanne, this is Loralin. Is Miles there?" If he were willing to answer her questions, she might not have to go to the inn at all that day.

"I'm sorry, Loralin," she said sweetly. "Miles is out until the day after tomorrow. He and the missus had to go up north for her son's track meets."

"Oh, well, okay, Joanne. I'll just catch him then. Thank you." Hanging up the phone, she couldn't help but remember the times when he'd missed their girls' events to chase a lead or work on a case. And now, here he was going to his stepson's events. But then again, he wasn't trying to beat out two other guys to become top detective now, as he had been. His competition at the time had been fierce.

Before she left the house to go talk to Jeffrey at the end of his shift, she left a message on Miles's personal voicemail. "Hey, Miles. I wondered if I could get the full list of people seen in the lobby the night of the murder. My copy is smudged. Thanks!"

The sun was still pretty low in the sky as she walked down the path to the hotel. Even Devin wasn't up and at work yet. Jeffrey would get off in twenty minutes, and she didn't want to have to chase him down, so she'd set her alarm for earlier than she'd like.

When she opened the door to the inn, she almost turned around and ran back home to hide under her bed. Utter Chaos was the only way to describe what she saw in the lobby. "What in the hell is going on here?"

"It's not my job to be doing cleaning and filing and checking people in," Jeffrey insisted loudly. "I'm tired of having to do it."

Loralin was puzzled. After the murder, everyone filled in where they were needed because no new guests were coming in. Now, however, things were back to normal in that aspect, and the bellhop had plenty of his own duties to keep him busy. "Why on earth are you still being asked to do extra jobs?" she asked. "Come on, let's go talk in my office."

Once they were settled in and Jeffrey was calmed down, holding a bottle of water, Loralin approached the subject again. "Care to tell me what was going on?"

Jeffrey shrugged, looking embarrassed at his outburst. "I'm sorry, Loralin. I didn't mean to get so upset. But when Malina and Roscoe didn't show up for their shift again, I got overwhelmed. This isn't what I signed up for. I mean, I'm happy to help out once in a while, but this is getting ridiculous."

Loralin felt for the poor guy. Since the murder, they'd had a higher turnover than she'd expected for the first couple of months. The beginning was always the hardest time for that. "When you say again, how many times have they been gone?"

"About three times this week. And at least one or two days other weeks."

This was all news to Loralin. Why hadn't Devin come to her with this? "Jeffrey, go on home and enjoy your days off. I'll see you in a couple of days, and I promise things will be better."

"Thank you, Loralin," he said with relief in his eyes. "I'm sorry for the outburst."

She stood to see him out. "Next time, come straight to Devin or me, okay?"

Pulling the door open, he nodded and started to leave.

"Wait, Jeffrey."

"Yes, ma'am?"

"I have a favor to ask." This was where she always turned on the charm.

"Sure. Anything." He looked puzzled but eager to please.

"Could you give me a list of people you saw around the hotel the night of the murder?"

"But… but I gave that to Detective Robbins."

"Yeah," she said, putting her arm around his shoulder and steering him out to the lobby. "But this is my house, and I just kind of need to know who was here. Can you do that for me?"

"Sure, Loralin. The shift is over, so can I text it to you? I need to get back to the house so my girlfriend can head to work. We share a car."

*****

A half-hour later, Loralin's phone beeped with a message from Jeffrey. She didn't get a chance to look at it before Devin burst into the room.

"Loralin, we have to do something about Melina and Roscoe. They are always calling out, but they bring doctor's notes. Everyone here knows they aren't sick. They see them hanging out at the bars and going Alcova reservoir outside of Casper."

"Ah, yes. I learned a bit about those two from Jeffrey earlier. How come this is the first I've heard of it?"

Devin looked down at his hands, which were grasped in front of him. "Well," he hesitated. "They had doctor's notes, and you were stressed and busy. I wanted to try to handle it myself, but I'm not sure what to do. If we fire them with the notes in their file, wouldn't we be in for a world of hurt?"

"Technically, not legally," she said softly. "But it is my personal policy, so it's a really gray area."

"Okay. I'm sorry, Loralin."

She smiled and looked at him. "I should thank you for being so kind as to think of me and my stress levels. But now it's time for you to get a lesson in small-town American employment. Do you have the doctor's name?"

"It's in the file," he said, moving over to where they kept their employee files. It only took a minute to get the name. "It's Doctor James Connor."

"That old bastard," Loralin murmured. "He'd give a doctor's note to a goat if he thought it's baas were them asking him for one. Watch and learn, my friend."

Devin sat in the chair in front of her desk and watched as she picked up the phone. For some reason, he couldn't wait to see what she did next.

"This is Doctor Connor's office. How may I help you?" A kind older woman answered the phone. Mrs. Connor had worked with her husband for as long as she could remember.

"Hey Doreen, this is Loralin Robbins. I need to talk to James. It's about a couple of my workers."

The older woman hemmed and hawed. "He's busy with a patient."

"Come on, Doreen, I'm not stupid. It's six thirty in the morning. He doesn't see patients until eight."

"Hold on," the older woman said. Loralin thought sometimes even she was tired of her husband's bull.

"Hello, this is Doctor Connor."

"Doctor Connor, this is Loralin over at the Robbins' Nest Inn."

"Well, hello there, to what do I owe the pleasure?" His voice betrayed him. He sounded nervous, not kind or helpful.

"If you ever give my employees fake doctor's notes again, I will report you to the medical board." Her voice was fierce and strong. This was the closest that Devin had ever come to hearing her yell. "We have pictures and videos of them partying and being active when they are supposed to be hurt or too sick to come to work. Hell, I might even contact the insurance board so they can see if you've ever lied to them!"

There was a long moment of silence on the line. She sure hoped her verbal thrashing hadn't caused the old man health issues. But then he spoke. "You won't see another note."

"Thank you," she said triumphantly and then hung up.

Devin was chuckling when the phone was rested back in its cradle. "Impressive."

Loralin also chuckled. "You haven't seen anything yet."

Ten minutes later, she had Malina and Roscoe, siblings that she used to babysit when they were young, on the line. "Okay, you two. No more notes from Doctor Connor. You either show up to work or provide an honest doctor's note. If you don't, you're fired!"

"I don't need that stupid job," Roscoe said. "You don't have to fire me, I quit."

"Yeah, me too," Malina said. "Sorry, Loralin. Daddy made us get the jobs. We didn't want to."

"It's okay," she said. "Come in and get your final paycheck tomorrow." She hung up the phone and laughed.

"Why are you laughing?" Devin said. "We are now two housekeepers short!"

"Because I knew that would happen, and I am so relieved. Those two are the most spoiled pair on this earth. I'm relieved they're gone."

"Yeah, but,"

Loralin interrupted him with a raised hand. Here is a list of four people who have applied and are qualified for the positions that just opened. Pick two you like and hire them. We need them to start the day after tomorrow."

Devin couldn't quite get himself to stand up out of the chair. "You're letting me hire them?"

"Of course," Loralin said with a smile. "It's part of your job, so what better time to start doing it than now?"

"Yeah," he said, looking directly into her eyes. "But I just messed up big time."

Loralin laughed again. "I wouldn't call it messing up. You just didn't quite know how I deal with things. Now you know. We're all good."

Devin stood up and left his boss's office. Damn, he loved working for her. She could be a pain in the ass, but when it came down to it, she was honest and fair."

*****

Loralin headed back home for a while after she was done at the inn. It would still be a couple of hours until her lunch date with her girlfriends, Marybeth and Rhonda. It had been a long time since she'd felt like going out at all. Of course, when she'd been planning and refurbishing the inn, she'd barely had time to take a shower some days, let alone hang out with her friends. The one exception had been Devin. She'd loved video chatting with him while working.

The one thing that worried her about the meet-up was how Ronda was going to treat her. They'd been the top sellers and partners in a real estate firm based throughout central Wyoming. The other woman hadn't been happy when Loralin had backed out to live her dream of reopening her grandparents' inn. It was something she'd had to do, though.

Why did this luncheon worry her so much, though? Rhonda was always such a pain in the ass, trying to outdo everyone. She was a friend, though, and she hated the thought that it could end just because she'd had the guts to do something for herself. Now, she wanted to talk to Devin.

"This is Devin. How can I help you?"

"Hey, Dev." She wasn't sure what to say yet.

"Loralin? Are you still worried about seeing Rhonda today?"

"Yeah. How did you know?" She didn't even really need to

ask that. It was just one of those things that happened with them.

"I know you. Please don't worry, Loralin. Do you think maybe things would have ended sooner if it was going to end?"

"Yeah, maybe," she said. "Maybe it's not the end of the friendship that I'm worried about. Maybe it's the haughty attitude about what I'm doing now compared to what I used to do."

Devin chuckled over the line. "And there you have it. You know how she is, and you know how she reacts to things. You can either defend yourself or let it go. Either way, I think you'll end the day as friends."

Once again, she felt better after talking to Devin. What would her anxiety be like without him? "Thanks, Bestie! I'm going to go get a shower and head out. I'll talk to you tonight. Love you."

"Love you too, Loralin."

*****

Loralin stood in the entryway to the little salad and sandwich shop downtown, next to the police station. It was the only place in town that Rhonda would eat because she didn't want to 'get fat' eating at 'greasy spoons'. She spied her two friends looking over the menu and chatting quietly. All seemed okay with them, so she moved into the dining area of the restaurant and headed for their table. "Hello, ladies. How are you today?"

"Hey!" Marybeth said as she stood for a hug. "I'm great. How are things at the inn?"

"Hello, darling," Rhonda said with a genuine smile. "Do tell us how your little inn adventure is going."

Loralin suddenly wondered how many times her beautiful business would be called quaint that day. "The inn is doing great. I think the murder actually helped. I'd just be better if we knew who had done it and could get on with our lives."

"It must be dreadful!" Rhonda said. "Wondering if the person is going to strike again."

"I'm not too worried," Loralin said, looking out the window at her rental car. "I just wish I knew why they'd chosen Penny. Everybody loved her."

"Except for that dreadful Austin. He only loved himself," Rhonda added. "I'm surprised it wasn't him."

"He was in jail," Lauralin informed her. Rhonda had no room to talk about Austin. She'd dated him off and on through high school.

"Well, I'm not surprised," Marybeth cut in. "We all know what a jerk he was. I'm surprised Penny got hooked up with him. He's like twelve years older than her."

Loralin was looking at the menu when she felt a hand on hers. "Shh, Marybeth. Don't talk bad about May/December relationships. You might offend Loralin."

"Really, Rhonda?" Loralin asked. "You know damn well that there is nothing between Devin and me!"

Rhonda sat back in her seat and smiled between her friends. "I think you're protesting too much. I was just joking."

Marybeth motioned the waiter over and turned to Rhonda. "You, my friend, need to stop. It's obvious that it's a touchy subject with Loralin after what his mother pulled. She went through hell for months."

"That woman is something else," Rhonda said. "I've seen her in action, and she is hateful and spiteful. I just wanted to hit her, and you know me, I like angry people."

Loralin took a moment to order her sandwich and let the others order their stuff, then she stared Rhonda down.

"How on earth would you know anything about Catherine Wentworth?"

"I've seen her around. She comes in on the hotel shuttle every other day or so."

"Oh." This was a surprise to Loralin. She hadn't noticed too much of what Devin's mom had done there for a while. "So, how was she acting?"

"Well, the one time that sticks out to me," Rhonda started. "She was on the phone, and she was cursing you up one side and down the other. Saying how much she hated you and how much she wished she could just get through to her son. You, my friend, make her livid."

"Well," Loralin said with a shit-eating grin. "You must not have seen her recently. She has been as sweet as pie, as my grandma used to say. We even spent the day in Casper shopping together."

Rhonda paused with her cup halfway to her mouth. "Really?"

"Yes. She decided to ease up a bit. It seems like she's accepted me." Loralin hoped it was true, although she was ever the skeptic.

"I swear it was just last week," Rhonda said, a look of confusion coloring her face."

"No, couldn't be," Loralin said. "She's been nice now for about that long."

Ronda shrugged and nodded her head. "It could be, hun. I just don't know. I sold four houses and two businesses in the last week. I have been slammed lately. It could have been a month ago, and I wouldn't remember."

Loralin felt the need to lighten the mood. "Ah, so that's why my leaving our partnership didn't hurt our friendship. You're making bank without me there!"

Rhonda grabbed Loralin for a sitting hug. "You know me so well." The three women laughed and dug into the food that their waiter brought.

18

Dinner Parties & Murderous Girlfriends

A messed-up food delivery to the inn had created a long day for Loralin and Devin. Miles and Meredith had invited them over for dinner, and she was curious as to why. That curiosity was the only thing that kept her from rescheduling. "You ready?" she asked her housemate as she walked into the living room.

"Yeah. Let's go get this over with." Devin said before a big yawn took his breath. "Are you sure you don't know what he wants?"

"I'm sure," Loralin stated. "Maybe he just wants to get to know you better. He always worries about me still. And of course, he worries about the girls and how you being here might affect Heather."

Devin nodded. "I know. But he doesn't have to worry. Heather and I are both fine. No feelings even developed, and think we might even end up friends again."

"I hope so," she said with a smile as she pulled on his hand to get him up out of his chair. "Let's go."

The car ride to the Robbins' house remained quiet as each of them contemplated what the evening would be like. It wasn't until they walked in the front door that they realized why they were there.

"Oh, thank God you're here. Come in, Miles is bouncing off the walls and driving me nuts. He needs someone to go over the case with him."

"Ah," Loralin realized. "So we're here so he can pick our brains and talk things out."

"Glad to be of service," Devin said with less than full confidence. "I think."

*****

"Come in, come in," Miles said as they stepped into the living room. "Sit down. Can we get you something to drink?"

"Iced tea if you've got it," Loralin said.

"I'll have the same," Devin decided. They both sat on the couch while Meredith left the room to get their drinks. "So how can we help?"

Miles smiled impishly. "Well, I realized that Jackie doesn't have enough of a background on the case since she was gone, and I need someone to bounce ideas off of. I've got to get this one solved as soon as possible."

Meredith came back into the room and set their teas on the coffee table. "Don't let him fool you. He misses having you help on his cases because, honestly, I have no interest in it, and if I did, I would be horrible at it."

"Nonsense," Miles grumbled as he reached down beside his chair and picked up a folder that contained case files. "I just want to see if I'm missing anything."

"Well, let's discuss this over dinner because I'm going to serve it now." Meredith stood and led the way to the dining room.

"So, where are you getting stuck the most?" Loralin asked as Devin held her seat out for her.

"Suspects," Miles stated. "We know the killer is a woman."

Devin thought for a moment. "If the killer is the same one who tried to take out Loralin, we know they are good with cars or know someone who is."

"So," Loralin said excitedly. "We need to keep an open mind that it could be more than one person."

Miles groaned loudly, and when Loralin and Devin looked up from their plates, he was sitting at the end of the table with his head in his hands. "I don't need another suspect, I just need one."

Loralin felt for her ex-husband. He said exactly what she'd been thinking. "Okay, let's start at the beginning. Someone surprises Penny in the parking lot and stabs her in the back. They walk into the woods and dispose of the gloves and robe. Let's start with the back door. How many of the fingerprints on the back door were those of women?"

Miles shuffled through some papers in his files and started to read. "Let's see here. There were five that belonged to men and three that belonged to women. There were many more that couldn't be determined because they were smudged or partial."

"Is it going to be a waste of time to go down that road?" Devin asked

"Maybe," Loralin said. "But for now, it's all we've got. "I think we should compare the names on that list with the names of those that Jeffrey saw out and about in the inn that night."

"It's a slim shot of coming up with something, but I agree with Loralin," Miles said. "It's worth looking at."

Loralin pulled up the list that Jeffrey had sent to her phone and read them off while Miles compared them to his list of fingerprints. In the end, there were only two matches: Lisa Marie and Catherine.

"Wait a minute," Devin said. "Lisa Marie was seen in the hotel? How is that possible? The bartender said she was at the bar with Chloe until last call."

Loralin picked her phone back up and scrolled through the list Jeffrey had given her. "It says here he saw her by the supply room on the second floor at about 2 a.m."

"Last call is at 2," Miles said. And the bar on County Road is a ways out there. Either the bartender is lying for her, or he's blind."

"Who was the bartender that night?" Loralin asked.

"Miles looked over his documents to find the statement from the man. "Riley Brandt."

"Yeah," Loralin said with a sigh. "He's usually drunker than the patrons."

"Come on, guys, you are really damaging the professional caterer's ego here. Can you at least eat some of the food I made?"

They all looked down at their nearly full plates and started to apologize all at once. Meredith just laughed it off. She was used to it.

The conversation strayed from the murder until everyone was finished with the main course. "That was truly wonderful, Meredith," Miles said. "As always."

"Thank you, dear," she said, smiling at her husband. "And now I will serve dessert, and you guys can talk all you want. I'm going to my book club meeting." She left the room to pull dessert out of the fridge.

"I'm going to make a call to the bar before we start dessert,"

Miles said as he got up from the table and stepped out of the dining room.

"I'm going to call my mother," Devin said. "Why in the hell was she roaming around the hotel in the middle of the night?"

While the two men were making their calls, Loralin decided to text Jeffrey. "Hey, where did you see Catherine Wentworth the night of the murder?"

He almost immediately replied. "I caught a quick glimpse of her coming into the lobby from outside right before the elevator door closed. And then I caught a glimpse of her on the third floor, going into her room."

"Do you know what time that was?" she texted.

"I'm going to say somewhere between three and four. I can't be sure, though."

"Thanks."

By the time Loralin had put her phone away, the two men were done with their calls. "Okay, who goes first?"

Miles didn't hesitate to speak up. "I talked to Riley. He said he saw Lisa Marie get up and head toward the bathroom about an hour and a half before last call, and then he remembers seeing Chloe gather up her stuff and Lisa Marie's purse and head out at about three. He'd just assumed that Lisa Marie headed to the car first."

"Damn," Devin said through clenched teeth. "Is my girlfriend really a murderer?"

"Your girlfriend?" Loralin asked. "When did this happen?"

Devin looked a bit embarrassed. "Yesterday, after she forgave me for leaving her at the accident site."

"Oh." Loralin wasn't quite sure what to think. Lisa Marie was a nice girl, at least she had been. She wasn't so sure anymore. "Well, I talked to Jeffrey. He said he saw Lisa Marie around two, about half an hour after the murder. She was by the supply room on the second floor."

"Yes," that matches the statement he gave us," Miles said as he went through his files. "Did you ask about Devin's mum?"

"Yeah. He said he saw a glimpse of her coming into the hotel through the closing elevator doors, and he saw her going into her room on the third floor, and this was between three-thirty and four."

Miles looked at his file and made a note. "We didn't have a time on here."

"And that corroborates what my mother just told me," Devin said as he sat at the table and took a bite of his dessert. He wasn't sure what it was, but it was delicious. "My brother sleepwalks, and my mother followed him downstairs during that time frame. I guess he went outside and started walking toward Loralin's house. She got him turned around and herded him back upstairs to bed."

"Did Jeffrey see Trevor with her?" Loralin wondered. "I'll ask him."

One quick text told them that Jeffrey hadn't seen the boy, but the glimpses were so fast that he could have been behind her or ahead of her, and he wouldn't have known.

"Okay, now let's just assume that my accident is related to Penny's death. Do either of these women know anything about cars? Did they hire someone?"

"Well, Lisa Marie's father wasn't just a good teacher and driving instructor," Miles informed them. "He was also a car junkie and a mechanic. That's how he paid for school."

"Oh," Loralin said, surprised. "I never knew that."

"Yep. And he taught his kids everything he knew about cars," Miles said. "What about your mum, kid? Does she know anything about cars?"

"No," Devin said. "My father always takes care of the cars. She even gets mad at him if he comes inside all greasy and smelly. He started keeping a change of clothes in the shed so he could change before he came inside."

"I hate to say this," Miles said, looking at Devin with a sympathetic look. "I think we might have a suspect. If your mother's story checks out, and with the fact that she didn't even know Penny, she should be cleared quickly. Lisa Marie, on the other hand, has some explaining to do."

"Yeah," Devin groaned. "Damn it, maybe she was lying when she said she wasn't jealous of Penny getting the management position. I feel like such a fool!"

*****

"You okay?" Loralin asked as she peeked into Devin's room the next morning.

"Yeah. I will be at least. I have no idea how to act around Lisa Marie today. I don't want to hurt Miles's case, but I feel like I should talk to her about it. I can't just ignore her."

Loralin walked all the way into the room and sat next to him. She grabbed his hand. "Miles will be questioning her this morning, so by the time she gets to work, it will all be out in the open. Just take it one step at a time and see how it goes."

Devin squeezed her hand. "Okay. Thanks once again, Loralin."

"For what?"

Devin smiled and stood up. "For everything. For calming me down, for being a friend, for helping me navigate life."

"You don't have to thank me," she said with a shy smile. "It's what friends do."

"Yeah. I hope I do the same for you." He put both hands on

her back and pushed her toward the door. "Now scoot so I can get dressed."

"Oh, but I wanted to watch," she teased as she closed his door.

"Pervert!" he called out. "I'm just a kid. And you're an old lady!"

Loralin laughed, and then she felt so bad. She didn't know why they flirted or talked like they did. They would never act on it. She didn't want to act on it. But flirting with Devin was fun; it was safe. That right there was her answer as to why. She didn't have to worry about him coming on too strong or trying to kiss or touch her when she didn't want him to. Dating had never been fun for her at all. Every time she'd flirted, they thought she immediately wanted more. Devin was different. She could be her flirty self without worrying about what would happen next.

*****

Devin was a mess. Had he really started to fall for a murderer? All morning, he'd been trying to think of tasks that he could do to keep himself out of the front of the hotel, maybe something in Loralin's office. But when Lisa Marie walked into the hotel at ten o'clock, he was standing at the front desk. "Devin, can I talk to you for a second?"

"Sure. I could use a break." He led her over to one of the loveseats, looking out at the mountains. "So, what's wrong?" He could tell she'd been crying.

"The police think I murdered Penny." Devin's eyes left her and wandered downward toward his lap. "You knew?" The tears started again.

"Yeah, I'd heard. How come you lied about your alibi?" Of all the stupid things to do, she'd done plenty that night.

"Because I knew how it would look if I told them I left the

bar early to come to the inn and get my ring." She pulled a tissue out of her sweater pocket and dabbed her eyes.

"Your ring?" he asked. "What ring?"

She showed him her right hand and the ring she always wore on her index finger. "My dad gave it to me when I was a little girl. I hardly ever take it off. But that day I did when I had to put my hands in cleaner. And then I was in such a hurry to go out with Chloe and celebrate our first day that I forgot it."

"Then why didn't you just stop by on your way home after last call?" None of it made sense. She was genuinely upset, but was she faking or not? He realized he just didn't know her well enough. Maybe he'd jumped the gun. Maybe he'd been just a little bit lonely for female companionship.

"When Chloe called her loser boyfriend to come join us for the last hour or so, I ditched her. I really hate that guy." Lisa Marie had stopped crying, and now she was getting angry.

"Okay, then why did you disappear out the back of the bar?" Devin remembered Miles saying the bartender thought she'd gone to the restroom, which was near the back exit.

"I always park in the back. You can ask anyone," she nearly cried. "I park out there, so after the bar closes, Riley can walk me out, and sometimes, I can get him to come home with me. Before I met you, of course."

"Of course." Devin wanted to believe her, but he just wasn't sure if he could yet. "Did anyone notice your ring missing? Someone who could back up your reason for coming back here?"

"Yes," she said with tears in her eyes again. "Riley noticed when he handed me a drink."

Devin nodded. "Okay, let's get you to the dining room and get some food and drink in you. Then when you're feeling better, head on up to work." He had his hand at the small of her back and was moving her forward when he suddenly stopped.

"What's wrong, Devin?" Lisa Marie stopped and turned to him.

"If you came back here at that time, how come you didn't see the body in the parking lot?"

Lisa Marie closed her eyes and swayed on her feet. "I don't feel very good, Devin."

He reached out for her and swept her up in his arms as she started to fall. "Someone call 911!"

*****

When Lisa Marie came to, Devin, Loralin, and Miles were all in her hospital room. "What happened?" she said, her voice scratchy.

Devin, who was sitting beside the bed, reached for a cup of water and handed it to her. "You passed out at the inn. Sweetheart, Miles needs to ask you some more questions."

She handed the cup back to Devin and nodded her consent. "Go ahead, Detective."

Miles moved up to the bed, and Devin stepped back to where Loralin was standing by the door. "Can you two excuse us?"

"No," Lisa Marie objected. "I want them here. Please."

Miles nodded his consent and turned back to his suspect. "Lisa Marie, did you see the body of Penny Carlisle when you came back to the inn to retrieve your ring?"

The tears started again, but she was fully in control this time. "Yes. I did."

"Did you see anyone in the area while you were in the parking lot?" Miles asked. He had the ultimate detective's voice.

Lisa Marie tried wiping her tears, but more just came behind the first. "Yes. I saw someone running away from the parking lot. I just didn't say anything because I was scared."

"What happened after you saw this person?" Loralin asked as she moved closer to her ex-husband. A dirty look from Miles didn't deter her, though.

"I went into the inn, and I got my ring and hurried home. I called Chloe and asked her to be my alibi because I was scared, not because I did anything wrong. I was terrified that someone would come after me next. The person heard my car pull in and looked back once as she ran away."

"She?" Miles asked. "You got a good enough look at this person to know it was a woman?"

Lisa Marie shook her head as it rested on the back of the pillow. "No. I guess I just assumed it was a woman because I think they had a ponytail over their shoulder when they turned toward the sound of my car."

"Did you see any features of the face?" Miles was trying to hide his excitement.

"No, they had a hoodie on, pulled low. The ponytail was the only thing that peeked out."

"Can you describe what this person was wearing?" he asked, his excitement momentarily under control. Only his ex-wife could see it now.

"The hoodie, A hotel robe, dark pants, and dark shoes."

"Were they tall, thin, short, fat?" Miles coaxed. "Any other characteristics that might help us figure out who this is?"

"Medium height, I'd say; taller than me for sure. And medium build too, although I'm not a hundred percent sure because the robe is bulky."

"Come on, people, it's time to let this lady rest. You can ask her more questions later." The nurse had come in and started shooing them out. It was time for her to take Lisa Marie's vitals.

Once in the hallway, the trio decided to head across the street to the little café that catered to guests of the hospital. Boone's small hospital didn't have the best food.

*****

"I believe her," Devin said as he took a bite of his hamburger. "I don't think she could make up all of that."

Miles nodded his agreement while he chewed his food and took a drink. "While they were assessing Lisa Marie, I took the info Devin gave me and called the bar. Riley remembers clearly that she didn't have her ring on, and he gave us the name of the guy who overheard their conversation about it, and he corroborated the story. Even if I still wanted her as a suspect, I don't think I'd have enough to go any further with her."

"So," Devin said with a sigh. That leaves my mother. Have you questioned her yet?"

"Yes," Miles said. "Your brother remembers waking up just as she tucked him in after the sleepwalk. And your father remembers hearing her leave and talking calmly to your brother."

"So," Loralin said with a sigh. Even though we have somewhat of a description of the person, we are back to square one."

"I'm afraid so," Miles agreed. "Damn it. I was hoping to have this case solved before the end of the month." It went unsaid that they were all happy that neither of the women was a suspect anymore.

19

Horses At The Inn

Once Loralin and Devin accepted the fact that they would probably never find the murderer, they started to enjoy the inn more. The murder was something that had happened, and the act itself was the end of the story. It was time to move on.

It was three days before the Wentworth family was to leave the country when Loralin got the call she'd been waiting for. The local farmer who hosted their guests on horseback riding treks was retiring, and his kids were turning the place into a soybean farm and only needed to keep a few of the horses. The farmer gave her the remaining ten horses for a great price. They would be delivered the next day.

Loralin woke up with the sun, as excited as a kid on Christmas. The stables at the back of the property had seemed such a waste sitting there empty, with guests passing it daily for hikes and other excursions. She couldn't count the number of times people had asked why she didn't just have horses here instead of shipping everyone off to the other farm. "Good morning," she said when she heard Devin pad into the kitchen behind her.

"Good morning," he returned. "I take it you're excited about the horses."

"You know I am," she said with a laugh. "And, I know you're not as excited."

Devin didn't want to go into why he didn't like horses. But he knew she'd bring it up and tease him like always. "You know, horses and I don't get along."

"It's not that, and you know it," Loralin corrected. "You got bucked off once and have been afraid of them since. You need to try again. You're not a little kid anymore, you won't go flying twenty feet anymore. Hell, with your adult weight and height, you might only go a couple of feet."

"You're so mean," he said with a fake pout. "I don't want to go any amount of feet if it is because of a damn horse."

Loralin shook her head, feigning disappointment. "I'm going to have you riding with me in no time."

"Nope," he said, taking his coffee with him as he headed back to his bedroom. "Never ever, Loralin. You hear me?"

"Oh, I heard you," she said softly to no one in particular. "But I don't always follow the rules, my friend. You should know that by now."

*****

Loralin was in her office when she was notified that the horses had arrived. When she arrived at the stables, there was already a crowd of guests gathered. And even Devin was there. He didn't look like he felt so good. "Why are you here?" she asked him.

"I just wanted to make sure the horses and I have an understanding. They stay away from me, and I'll stay away from them."

"That's gonna be hard to do once you start your riding lessons," she hollered as she walked away toward the driver of the horse trailer.

"What do you mean?" he hollered back.

"She means, not only did I teach you to drive, but I am going to teach you how to ride a horse." Lisa Marie stood looking up at him with a huge smile on her face.

"Oh, Hell no!" he said, backing away from her. "I refuse to get on one of those beasts." Just as he said that, one of the horses that had been unloaded in the first round nudged the side of his arm.

"Aww, hi girl," Lisa Marie said, reaching out to pat her. "See, she's not a beast, and she likes you."

The horse neighed and nudged him again. "Why is she doing that?"

"She likes you, dummy. Now just pet her like this." Lisa Marie took his hand and moved it along her snout.

"She likes this?" he asked.

"Yes." She removed her hand from Devin's and let him caress the beast next to him. "See, they aren't so bad, are they?"

This one was kinda sweet, but Devin wasn't going to admit it out loud. Yet.

*****

"Hey," Loralin said, walking up next to Devin. "I heard you made a new friend."

He shrugged. "Yeah, I guess. She was nosy like most women." His voice cracked with laughter, telling her he was just teasing.

"I should smack you for that." Loralin looked out over the yard where the horses were mingling before they headed to their stalls in the barn. "They are all so beautiful, but I think Emily is the prettiest."

Devin looked at her questioningly. "Emily?"

"Yeah. Your horse, the nosy one."

"Oh," Devin said. "I didn't know what her name was."

Loralin stood by her best friend and studied him. She sure hoped he was as happy as she was. She was almost afraid to ask because he didn't seem like he was in a talking mood. In the end, the words just didn't want to come out, so she remained silent about it. It wasn't often that they were at a loss for words around each other, but this seemed to be one of those times. He was in his own little world, so instead of saying something, she studied him. Had the horses bothered him that much? At this point, he even looked different somehow. "You okay?" she finally whispered.

"Yeah," he said softly. "Just tired and kind of weirded out by the horse, umm, Emily."

Something else was on his mind, but she wasn't sure what it could be. "Hey, I've never seen that jumper," she finally said to make conversation and draw him out of his funk.

"Uh, yeah, it's Mums. I didn't realize it had been packed in my bag. I'll have to give it back to her before tomorrow, I guess."

Loralin suddenly felt cold and wished she had a sweater or a jacket of her own. These early spring mornings could be chilly, especially with a breeze like today's. "Well, the stable hand that I hired from the farm will get the horses settled. I'm going to go back to the inn and check on things."

"Sure," he said with a smile. "I'll see you there later. I need to check on the landscape out front."

*****

Loralin knew it was cool outside, but she was downright freezing. Something kept creeping into her mind, and it seemed to make her colder. She couldn't stop shivering, so she ran to her house before she went to check on things at the inn. Grabbing a sweater, she filled a travel mug full of warm water from the kettle on the stove and put a tea bag in to seep while she called Miles.

"Hello, Loralin." He answered his cell phone on the third ring.

"Hey Miles, are you at the office? I'd like to come in and speak to you." Her mind was running so fast she couldn't figure out where to begin, but she always knew Miles was a safe place to start.

"I'm about ten minutes away. I can meet you there if you'd like."

"Yes, please." She thought she heard him say something as she hung up. But she didn't have time to worry about it. She needed to get to the police station as soon as possible. The inn would have to wait."

Loralin was so glad she had her SUV back. She really didn't like driving strange cars that many other people had used. As she drove to the police station, she went over the thoughts that had started to invade her mind. If she was right about what she was thinking, the world they lived in would never be the same. Mile's city-issued car pulled into the parking lot just moments after she did.

When they met up at the entrance of the building, Miles pulled her into a hug and kissed her cheek. "Is everything okay? You don't look so good?"

"Yeah, yeah, I'm fine," she said with a half-smile. "I just had some thoughts this morning, and they keep multiplying. I need to ask you some questions so I can put them to rest."

"Uh oh," Miles said, ushering her into his office. "Is this like you think you may have solved the case, type of multiplying thoughts?"

"Maybe," she relented. "I'm not entirely sure yet, though." She always had to be careful what she said to Miles. If she said the wrong thing, it could send her off on a wild goose chase. She had to stick to the basics.

"Okay, then. What would you like to know?" He was sitting behind his desk, and Loralin was pacing the floor in front of it.

"Can I look over the notes that you took after I made my copies? Please? I really need to get things together in my mind.

Miles handed her a file. "Don't tell anyone I let you see that."

Loralin smiled and sat down in a chair. "Thanks, there's more though."

"Go on," he encouraged with a wry smile. He'd been expecting more.

"Have you gotten any of the forensics stuff back yet?"

"A few things. Why?" Now he sounded skeptical.

"Is there any way I could sneak a peek?"

Miles's office phone rang, and he picked it up. "Yes? Okay, I'll be right there."

Loralin looked expectantly at him, and he nodded and pointed to a file on his desk. "Thank you."

"I know nothing, you say nothing." He left the office and closed the door.

*****

Loralin was writing the last of her notes when Miles returned to the office. "Here you go." She handed him his files. "And thank you so much, Miles. I owe you one."

"Care to share what you found?" he asked as she reached the door to his office.

"Not yet," she said with an apologetic smile. "I have a few

things to look into, then you'll be the first to know."

Miles sighed and plopped down in his seat. "Alright. Just be careful if you start accusing people."

"I always am," she said as she walked out and closed the door behind her.

"No, you're not," he grumbled to himself as he opened some files and started to read.

*****

Loralin hurried home and shut herself in her bedroom with a pen, a notepad, the files she had from the murder, and her cell phone. She had a murder to solve, and she wanted to do it as quickly and efficiently as possible. Her first call was to Don Peterson in Cheyenne.

"Hello, this is Don." The chief sounded tired and worn down.

"Don, this is Loralin. How are you?"

"Loralin! It's great to hear from you." His tone perked up at once. "How are you doing after the accident?"

"I'm doing great, Don," Loralin said in her sweetest voice. "I'm so sorry about the concert."

"Don laughed his good-natured laugh. "That's alright. It's not like you could help what happened. Have they found out who did it?"

Loralin had a feeling she knew, but she had to connect some dots first. "They still don't know if it is related to the murder, but I think it is."

"Well, I hope you're staying safe," he said. "I'm assuming that you called for a reason other than to exchange pleasantries."

"I actually called because I had some questions about the shoe print evidence that is almost done being processed." She hoped he could help because she didn't know anyone at the state forensics lab.

"Well, I'd be happy to help if I can," he said warily. "Wouldn't Miles know as much as I do?"

Loralin had hoped he wouldn't ask that question. "Maybe, but I know you are closer to the state lab people, and truthfully, Don, I don't want Miles to know what I'm doing. He would just take things too far and hurt people I care about."

Don snickered. "Yeah, sounds about like the Miles I know. So, what is it you need to know?"

"The shoe prints, what were all of the kinds of shoes and sizes?" She heard Don shuffling papers on his desk.

"Well, it says here that they should have that information today. How about I call and see what they've got? That way, we don't have to wait for the report to be sent."

"Oh, Don, that would be great! Thank you. I'll talk to you soon." Loralin put her phone down and sat back against her headboard. Part of her hoped he had the information she needed, and the other part knew that if he did, lives would be forever changed.

She was in the kitchen making herself a glass of iced tea when Don called her back. "Hey, Don. Did you find out anything?"

"I have all the brands and sizes but for one. They have to do further research. It's not a common brand." She could hear Don moving papers around on his desk.

"And do we have sizes?" Loralin wasn't sure what size she was looking for, but in the end, she knew it would be important. She wrote the sizes down to coordinate with the brand of shoes and the suspected size of the unknown print. All she had to do was talk to some people around the hotel, and she would hopefully know who had murdered Penny Carlisle in the parking lot of the Robbins' Nest Inn.

20

Fishing For Evidence

Loralin had just come from town about an hour after talking to a few people at the inn about the case. She was now about eighty percent sure of who had killed Penny. All she had to do was prove it. Unfortunately, she had to do it soon, but she wasn't exactly sure how. Usually, she planned these things down to a T, but this go around, she didn't have the time. All she knew was that Miles had her back.

With a quick inner shrug, she walked through the door of her house. Devin was sitting on the couch in the living room with his parents and brother. "Hey, guys, what's going on?"

"We're going to go fishing while you and Mum hang out or do whatever girl stuff you want to do," Devin said as the men stood. "We'll meet back here in a couple of hours to get Mum and Dad and Trevor to the airport."

"Have fun, guys. If you catch something, Devin and I can have it for dinner tomorrow." Loralin walked them to the door and accepted a kiss on the cheek from her best friend. "Don't go far. You don't want to get stuck or bogged down and not get back in time to make it to the airport."

"Yes, boss," he said with a smile and ushered his father and Trevor out the door.

"So, what do ya want to do today?" Catherine asked. "I could show ya how to make some of Devin's favorite foods."

"Devin already said he'd show me," Loralin said sweetly. "But I'd love to discuss and write some of them down. You know, find out if there are any quirks to the recipes that I should know before I try to make them myself."

"Sure," she said. "That sounds like fun. And I can tell ya some funny stories about Devin. Then you'll really know what you're in for."

Loralin didn't like the way she'd said the last sentence. It was almost like the old Catherine had said it. "Okay, I'm going to go use the restroom. I'll meet you in the breakfast nook."

When she walked into the kitchen's small breakfast area, Loralin was carrying some clothes. "Hey Catherine, I noticed we're about the same size. If you have room in your suitcases, I have these hoodies I never wear, and I notice you wear a lot of them. Would you like to take them?"

Catherine looked up and smiled at her. "That's so very kind of you, but I only wear jumpers that are big on me. I usually just buy Devin's size or take his old ones." Her attention returned to the paper she had been writing recipes on.

Loralin shrugged and set the hoodies on the nearby counter. "That's okay, it was worth a shot. I don't like the color of these three on me, so I thought I'd ask. My Hanna might be able to wear them. Although man, I wish she'd get busy and give me a grandchild. I'd hold on to those hoodies until the end of time if it meant they wouldn't fit her because she's pregnant."

"Ah," Catherine said. You've been bitten by the grandma bug, too, huh?"

"Yes, I've probably been bitten by a hundred of them," Loralin admitted with a laugh.

"Same," Catherine said. "Do me a favor, if Devin finds a girl, don't interfere. Let him be with her and get me some grandkids."

Loralin didn't like how she'd said that sentence either. She would never interfere with Devin finding love and building a life. Would she? "Don't worry, Catherine. I'll make sure he gives you plenty of grandbabies. I'll only make him work a half day on his wedding day and half days for the honeymoon."

Catherine looked up at her in shock, then her expression lightened, and they laughed together. "Thank you for taking care of him when we leave."

"I think he can take care of himself," Loralin said. "He's a man now."

Catherine nodded her agreement. "I guess I'm just worried that he can't. He never really had to before. And ya know, he reminds me of his father in so many ways."

"Oh, really, do tell," Loralin suggested.

"Well, Mark had really never been on his own before. I had at least spent summers at my grandmother's, where there had been no supervision, and then I lived alone for a year or two working with my cousin."

"Oh really?" Loralin asked. "Devin never mentioned that. What did you do? Is that how you got into the hotel business?"

Catherine shook her head. "No, that was Mark's thing. I didn't get involved until I married him. My father was a mechanic, and so were my uncle and my cousin. I helped my cousin start his shop on the mainland."

"Oh, that's right," Loralin said, hoping her voice was calm. "That's what Mark told me when he, Trevor, and I had a little chat this morning."

Catherine put her pen down and pushed the paper away from her. "Could I trouble ya for a glass of water? I'm really thirsty."

By the time Loralin set the glass of iced water on the table, Catherine had stood and was looking out the window of the breakfast nook. "What else did Mark tell ya?" Her voice had changed again.

"Oh, nothing much. Trevor told me something interesting, though."

Catherine turned quickly to Loralin. "And I suppose you're going to tell me what he said." The bitter, angry, hateful woman had made her return. Loralin didn't expect her to leave again anytime soon.

"He told me that he hadn't been sleepwalking the night of the murder. In fact, he told me he hadn't done that in a few years. All he remembers is you tucking him in at some point."

"Oh, how would he know? He's only a child. And he rarely wakes up or remembers anything about sleepwalking," she huffed.

Loralin shrugged. "He also told me something else."

Catherine's hands were clenching and unclenching at her side. "And what might that be?"

"He said he was awake when you left the room, and that's how he knows he didn't sleepwalk."

It was like a switch suddenly flipped. "Oh, why do ya even believe him, or Mark for that matter? They all hate me. My whole family. I do my best for all these years, and all they do is bitch and complain that I'm mean, or bitter!" She was starting to get emotional on top of the anger she always seemed to feel.

"Catherine, did you kill Penny?" Loralin held her breath

waiting for the answer.

"What? You bitch! How can ya stand there and ask me that? Why would I kill that girl? I didn't even know her. We had Devin's girlfriend cleaning our room, so I'd only seen her maybe once or twice."

Loralin couldn't help but feel that someone was protesting a bit too much. "Why did you lie, Catherine? What is your actual alibi?"

"My alibi hasn't changed, ya tramp! Trevor is a child, and he doesn't know what he's talking about. He was sleepwalking, and I was following him. That's all! Ya have no real proof that I killed anyone."

"What about my car? You had the basic know-how to tamper with both brakes and what you didn't know you could pick up quickly off of YouTube." Loralin had two emotions running through her at that moment. One was fear, and the other was a version of sadness and devastation. If she was right about her assumptions, Devin's world would be upended, and it would be a long time before things would be right again.

"I don't have to tell you anything," Catherine seethed. "I can't believe you. First, you corrupt my son and continue to lie about it. And then you accuse me of murder and attempted murder? You are the evilest creature on this earth. I'm leaving. Send my husband and son to the inn when they get back. I'll hire a car, ya won't be needed to get us to the airport."

Loralin couldn't let her leave. Stepping in front of her best friend's mother, she took a deep breath and lied through her teeth. "I'm so sorry, Catherine. I didn't mean it. I just need to know who killed Penny. It's hard to enjoy my inn knowing that the killer is still out there. I want Devin to be happy, too."

Catherine seemed to relax a bit, but then she tensed up again.

"It's too late for apologies. You know, I'm going to tell Devin exactly what happened today. Do you think he'll love ya after he finds out you accused his mother of murder?"

Loralin was quickly losing her, and she wasn't done yet. When Catherine pushed ahead toward the living room and front door, she dashed ahead and blocked it with her body. "What about the shoe print? You do know that the shoes you wore that night are only made in Australia, right?"

Catherine stopped where she was. "What are ya on about?" Catherine asked. Her shaky voice betrayed her, however.

"You thought of just about everything else to hide what you were doing. You stole a robe and some gloves from the supply closet to cover your clothes. You had your hair and face covered by one of the oversized hoodies you wear. And then you washed it in my washer, dried it, and put it in with your son's clothes. Did you want Devin to get blamed? Maybe as payback for daring to leave you?"

"Ya stupid whore," Catherine screamed. "I would never hurt my son as you've hurt him." Her breathing was coming in such angry gasps that Loralin thought she might pass out.

"You should have borrowed someone else's shoes, though, Catherine. You left that one perfect size nine footprint right under the tree where you stashed the robe and glove."

"You don't know what the hell you're talking about. I guarantee the shoe you are describing won't be found in my luggage. You can go ahead and search it." She started moving forward again.

"What do you think they would have found in the drain of my washing machine?" Loralin wasn't surprised when Catherine stopped again. "Or how about the fact that you didn't wear your hair up when you did it, so Lisa Marie saw your ponytail hanging out of the hoodie. Oh, and then there is the little boy who heard two women yelling below his window. We didn't think to ask him if one of the women had an accent."

"Well, see then," Catherine snapped. "Ya have nothing on me. You'll find nothing on me. I'm leaving."

Loralin put her hand out and stopped the woman. "You didn't let me finish. We didn't ask the boy at the time of his initial questioning. We did, however, ask him when I was in town today. I wasn't surprised when he said that the woman who was yelling mean things had the same accent as the mermaids on the shows he watches. There are at least two popular mermaid shows with the kids these days. They are made in Australia and star actors from Australia."

Catherine seemed to slump forward, but then straightened herself. She had a gun in her hand, pointed straight at Loralin. "Ya should have just left it alone. That murder is making you the big bucks. You should just have left it alone and enjoyed the spoils."

Loralin slowly moved sideways away from the door. The gun followed her, but she felt better not being backed against something. "Are you sure you can use that gun?" she asked. "I mean, they aren't allowed in your country."

"My granddaddy taught me to shoot long before they were outlawed." She had a smile on her face that made her look like a maniac from a horror movie.

That was the last thing Loralin had wanted to hear. She was genuinely scared for her life now. She needed to keep Catherine's mind busy to keep her from thinking of shooting her. "So, where did you get that gun, and why did you have it with you if we were just hanging out?"

"I'll tell ya that when I think you need to know," she huffed.

"Right now, I need you to get your ass outside and get in the car. We're going to pick up my husband and sons, and you're taking us to the airport."

"What about your luggage?" She had to think of a way to stall her so Miles and his crew could make it there to arrest her. She didn't really feel like dying that day.

"It's already in the car. Devin had Mark do it so we could leave straight from here." Catherine's phone rang, and she kept a steady hand on the gun as she answered it. "Where are you guys?"

Loralin wished she could have heard what Mark said because the look on his wife's face was ten times worse than it was before the call. "What's wrong?"

When Catherine looked up, Loralin involuntarily took a step back. "We're going without them. They will have to find their own way. Damn, idiots got themselves bogged down."

Loralin led the way out to her SUV. Every step of the way, she prayed that her wire was still working and that Miles would show up soon or be able to follow her. Just as she was going to start the engine, her phone buzzed. "It's my daughter. She never calls this time of day. I have to answer it."

Catherine thought for a moment and motioned with the gun that she could go ahead. "Just don't say anything stupid."

"Hey, Hanna. Is everything okay?"

"Good way to hide who is calling," Miles said, his voice serious and calm. "I just wanted to let you know that we had an issue and couldn't get to you before she had you enclosed in the car. Don't worry, though, we are going to follow you."

"Well, that's a relief," Loralin returned. "I don't see how that's going to help save anyone, but if that's what you want to do, then I say do it."

"Okay, I promise we won't let anyone hurt you. Try to get her to tell you about the murder on the drive to Casper. We want to get the whole story. It will go better in front of a judge or jury if needed."

"Okay, sweetheart. I love you." She hung up the phone, wondering if she would ever hear Miles' voice again.

21

A Story To Tell

Loralin drove down the lane that led away from the inn and turned onto the highway. Within minutes, she saw the surveillance van following them. She hoped that Catherine wasn't aware of what it was. "Can you do me a favor, Catherine?"

"Oh sure, I'm all keen to do a favor for a bitch." The woman's smirk was strong as she turned to Loralin.

"Come on," Loralin said sweetly. "I just want to know about the murder. Why did you do it and how did you do it? I mean, I'm pretty sure I know. I could probably just tell the police my version. But I don't know, you might not like it."

Catherine looked scared of what her nemesis might say about her. "I stole the gun from that old man who wears them on his hip. He took it out when he sat down and set it on the end table. I grabbed it, and he didn't even notice it was gone."

"Mr. Weeber?" Loralin asked. "He was walking around this morning looking for it."

"Well, he ain't gonna find it. I needed it to kill ya before we left. My whole goal since you humiliated me in front of your dinner guests was to kill ya. I failed twice, and I wasn't about to leave here with your dumb ass alive."

"So," the realization hit Loralin hard. "You mistook Penny for me."

"Yeah," she said. "I thought I saw you go into your office when I was in the lobby because I couldn't sleep. I ran upstairs and grabbed the stuff I'd taken to disguise myself. I'd planned on doing it the next day, but figured I might as well do it while you were alone. So I hid in the stairwell and waited until who I thought was you came out of the office."

"But it wasn't me. Penny had gone into the office to leave her keys soccer we didn't have a lockbox yet." Loralin felt guilty, but she had to push it aside. She needed to concentrate on what was going on around her.

"Yes. You had been wearing the same shirts the housekeepers wear, and you had your hair in a braid, too. So, I followed her out, and I rammed the knife into her back as hard as I could. I was so angry. I was yelling at her and telling her what a horrible person she was. And then I realized it wasn't you." For a moment, Catherine almost sounded like she felt bad.

"You could have called an ambulance." Loralin wished like hell that she'd thought about that.

"I couldn't move," she admitted. "I must have stood there for fifteen minutes before someone drove into the car park, and then all I could do was run."

"Loralin almost felt bad for the woman. She did feel bad for Mark, Trevor, and Devin, though. "What made you throw the robe and gloves in the tree?"

Catherine looked out the window, but she still had the gun trained on Loralin. "I didn't know what to do with them. I did know not to throw them in a trash can, and that you didn't have the boiler running yet. So, I figured I'd hide them up high."

"Did you just throw them up there?" Loralin didn't believe she had, but she wanted to know. Her curiosity about everything crime-related sometimes threatened to get her into trouble.

"Hell no," Catherine grumbled. Her mean streak was coming back. "I'm perfectly capable of climbing a tree. I put them up there where they shouldn't have been able to fall."

"But you didn't know about the Wyoming wind," Loralin said.

"No," she admitted. "Did they find any DNA on it?"

"I don't know," Loralin admitted. "I haven't looked at those results yet."

"And the shoes," Catherine asked, once again sounding melancholy.

"They just have the print. Are you saying that the shoes are still around somewhere?" Loralin hoped they were because then they could match the soil and make the case more solid.

"I didn't realize how much mud was on my shoes until I got back to the inn. I knew I couldn't come in the back way without getting dirt everywhere, so I took them off and hid them in the flower bed when I came back in the front door. Once I got upstairs, I realized that some of the soil on my hands was red, so I took them to that old construction dumpster out past the stables and the pond before breakfast."

"That means they are still there," Loralin commented more for the mic she was wearing than for Catherine. "I haven't had that dumpster emptied since the refurb on the stables ended three months ago."

"Oh," was all Catherine said as she looked down at the gun

in her hands.

"So, what about my brakes?" Loralin asked after a few minutes of silence. "It was you who cut them, right?"

"I did," she admitted. "I was even angrier when it sank in that I'd killed someone, and you still weren't dead. So, I cut your brakes knowing that you were going on that mercy date with that police chief."

Loralin really felt bad for her. She didn't know how someone could hold so much hate in their heart. "And when that failed, you moved on to plan C, which included you pretending to accept me."

Catherine laughed harshly. "Yeah. I bet you think it was hard for me, but it wasn't. There's always been an aspect of you that I wanted to like, that I wanted to be friends with. So, I buried the hate and enjoyed myself for a while. But then, I just couldn't not do anything about you and leave here."

"So, you decided to bring a gun into my house to murder me before you fled back to Australia?"

"Yes, and I'm going to do it. I just haven't decided when. I don't know if I should do it the minute we pull into the car park or wait until Devin gets there so he can watch."

Suddenly, Loralin wasn't sure if she would do what she said or not. Would a mother do that, especially one who occasionally seemed to love her family despite how she treated them? "You don't have to do this, you know. "If you kill me, they kill you."

"Shut up! No one is going to know where we are except for my family."

Loralin had to make a decision, and it had to be the same one Miles would make in this case. "We're almost to the airport. Do you know where your family is?"

Catherine fished her phone out of her pocket and hit the speed dial. "Where are ya! Hurry up then."

"Are they close?" Loralin asked, hoping she had the right answer.

"About twenty minutes behind us. Lisa Marie is driving them."

Now was the time to make the move. She still prayed that Miles would agree it was the right thing to do. As soon as she was on the road to the airport, she made her move. "Your family and Lisa Marie won't be the only ones who know about this."

"The bitch," Catherine cut in. "I'm not really looking forward to killing her either."

"What I was saying before you interrupted me," Loralin said through gritted teeth. "Is that your family, and Lisa Marie won't be the only ones there. "I'm wearing a wire."

The hand holding the gun began to shake. "You cunt!"

"Please don't use that word here. And don't shoot me," Loralin reminded her. "I'm driving, and if you shoot me, we both go off the road."

Catherine seemed to lose a lot of steam in that moment. She was getting scared and would start to make mistakes, exactly what she was hoping for. "I need to think."

Loralin remained quiet as she turned into the airport and made her way to a parking spot. It wasn't until she turned the engine off that she spoke again. "You need to give yourself up before things end badly."

"I don't want to," she said. "This all got out of hand. It was just supposed to be you, and then I'd go home and live my life with my family, all of them, including Devin."

"I'm sorry," Loralin said softly. "I'll admit that it's pretty bad now, but please don't make it worse."

"Will you help me?" she was talking so softly that Loralin had to lean in to listen.

"Yes. Can you put the gun on the dashboard first? And then you need to let me call Detective Robbins."

Catherine slowly moved the gun forward and laid it on the dashboard. "Go ahead and call."

Loralin picked up her phone from the center console and dialed her ex-husband's number. "Miles, the gun is on the dashboard, and she's ready to give up. Can you tell her what you need her to do?" She put the phone on speaker.

"Hey, Mrs. Wentworth. I need you to look out the window and see the officers. Do you see them?"

"Yes."

Miles was using his comforting voice. He had a way of telling if someone was in distress. "I need you to open the door and put your hands in the air. Then I need you to walk slowly toward the officers. Can you do that?"

"Yes." She reached for the door and opened it. With her hands above her head, she left the vehicle. Within seconds, the police had her on her knees and were cuffing her. When Loralin looked toward a noise she heard coming from the entrance of the parking lot, she saw Devin, Mark, and Trevor standing on the pavement watching what was going on.

Loralin got out of the car and walked over to them. "I'm so sorry, Devin."

He looked at her and shook his head. "It wasn't your fault, but what exactly happened?"

"She wanted to kill me and got Penny instead. Then the car accident failed, and this was her last chance."

Devin stepped toward her and seemed to melt into her arms.

"I'm the one who's sorry, Loralin. I can't believe she would do something like that."

"I think she just got lost along the way," Loralin pointed out. It was the first time she'd ever seen Devin actually cry.

22

A New Beginning

Loralin walked along the bank of the river, now free of ice and flowing steadily. She soaked in every bit of warmth the cloudy day provided. She'd been cold for too long. Devin was with her, but walking a couple of feet behind. Ever since his mom's arrest, he'd been quieter than usual, and she completely understood why. In a way, he'd hated his mum for how she'd treated him, but deep inside, she was still his mother, and he loved that part of her. She stopped and waited for her best friend. "You okay?"

"Yeah," he said, looking out over the river. "I don't know if Dad selling the hotel and staying here is a good idea."

"Why not?" she was genuinely curious. "He just wants to be near you and your mom."

"I know," Devin agreed. "But he needs to be back home with his friends and his siblings and cousins and nieces and nephews. There's nothing here in America for him. I can take care of myself, and I can keep an eye on Mum."

Loralin knew he was right, but Mark was a grown man and could make decisions for himself. "You have to let him do what he feels he needs to do."

"Damn it!" Devin raged after a few minutes of silence. "Why did she have to do this? Why did she have to hate so much?"

Loralin knew better than to answer. Her biggest fear was that her friendship with Devin would end because of her role in getting his mother sentenced to prison in a foreign country. "Come on, it's time to get back to the house. Your dad wants to start looking for an apartment."

"Go on ahead, and I'll be right there." She knew it was time to leave him alone. He bent to pick up a rock and skipped it into the river. The ripples and the slight sound they gave as the rock moved downstream were always one of Loralin's favorite sounds. Perhaps Devin would find some comfort in it, too.

*****

Loralin took her time walking back to her cozy little house. It was the only haven she had at the moment. One thing kept playing over and over in her head. The possible initials AU that had been written in blood were Penny's way of telling them that someone from Australia had done it. How had she missed that? They'd been focused on names, of course, because one would usually name the person who had killed them, but in this case, Penny probably didn't remember her first name. Loralin decided she needed to read some more mystery novels; she'd gotten rusty in her break from detective sidekick after the divorce. But then again, would she ever need the skills again? She sure as heck hoped not.

In a way, Loralin felt lost despite the success of her hard work. Devin was a mess, his family was a mess, and the inn was abuzz with all the goings on about the upcoming trial. Nothing felt normal yet, and how long would it take her best friend to feel like he belonged there with her? He'd almost been to that point when his mother's arrest had ruined everything. She knew he thought daily about moving back with his father to help out in the hotel; One certain way to get his father to go home.

"Hey, Loralin. Are you guys ready to go? I hate taking up space in your house, and I want to find Trevor and me a place of our own."

"You guys are no trouble," she said, kissing Mark on the cheek. "But I understand what it's like to want your own place."

"You have to stop him," Mark said as he followed her to her SUV.

"Stop him?" she asked. "I'm not sure what you're talking about."

Mark got in the passenger seat and was quickly joined by Trevor, who had been following behind. "Stop him from going home and taking over the hotel. What he doesn't realize is that I don't want the damn thing; I never wanted it. Catherine insisted that I keep it and run it. I always liked the maintenance and lawn keeping and such much more than the day-to-day operations of the place."

That news was a surprise to Loralin. "Have you told him?"

"I tried," he admitted. "But he thinks I'm lying just to save his feelings. He loves it here and doesn't want to leave. He's going to, though, if we don't stop him."

Every time it was mentioned that Devin might leave, her heart broke into pieces. "Okay, here's what we're going to do. I need a new handyman when Josiah leaves. The job is yours when your work visa comes through if you want it."

"Really?" Mark asked. "That would be amazing." He was more excited than Loralin had ever seen him.

"Yes. And then you have to fib just a bit."

Mark's excitement dimmed. "About what?"

"Tell him the hotel has already sold. There will be nothing for him to drag you back to." Loralin held her breath, hoping he would agree.

Five minutes ticked by, and Devin was finally seen walking out of the woods surrounding the river. "Okay. I'll do it." Mark was on board, so now Devin would be staying. Loralin only felt a little bit bad about the lie.

*****

Devin wasn't so sure about his father working at the inn. Should the former owner of a successful but small local hotel move down to a general caretaker? "Are you sure, Dad?"

"Yes," Mark said, strapping his new tool belt around his waist. "This is what I enjoyed most about our hotel. Think back, Dev. Remember."

He had to admit that his father was right. Mark had always been working on one project around the place or another while he and his mother ran the business side of things. And his dad looked so happy, even though his wife was awaiting trial on a murder charge. Maybe Loralin had been right, and this was a good thing for all of them. Thank goodness the work visa had come through quickly for his father. And Trevor would be starting school at Elk River Middle School in a few days. "Alright, Dad, we'll give it a try."

"That's my boy! Now, if you'll excuse me, I've got to get to work."

"And I have to get to Lisa Marie's." Devin was now steadily dating the older housekeeper.

"Have fun, son. Are you sure you love this girl?" Mark was unsure. He'd always preferred a different woman for his son.

"I like her a lot, Dad," Devin said with a smile. He hated

talking about love and relationships with his father. "That's all I can say for now. We are still early in the relationship. See ya later."

*****

Loralin had kid-sitting duty for the day. Trevor was in her office playing a video game with one of the guests of the hotel. "Hey, kiddo, you guys doing okay?"

"Yes, ma'am," he said politely. "You don't have to worry about us. I'll stay here until Dad gets off work."

Loralin knew he would keep his word, so she ducked back out to the front desk, where Mr. Walden stood waiting. "Well, hello, Mr. Walden. Are you and the family back for another stay?"

"Not this time, Mrs. Robbins. I just wanted to stop in and say thank you for all the help when we were here before. My ex-wife was killed in a car accident last week, so we can live freely again. We're going to go stay with my pops for a while and probably get our own place in the area here soon."

Loralin smiled widely. "Great! We're so happy to have you here. Give my best to your wife and Elliot."

"Will do and thank you again." He turned and walked out the door. One thing Loralin loved about the inn was that she got to share in people's lives, people whom she otherwise would never get to know.

"Loralin," Chef's voice assaulted her, but not in French.

"Is something wrong, Pierre?"

"I'm just not feeling it today. I've put the kitchen in the hands of Terry, and I'm headed home."

Loralin didn't like how he looked. If he were sick, maybe it would be better if he went home. "I hope you're feeling better soon."

"Oh, I'm not sick," he said grimly. "My ex-wife has a meeting scheduled here today, and I will murder the bitch if I see her right now."

After Chef walked toward the employee break room, Loralin got her composure back and turned to Maureen. "Who is his ex-wife?"

"Phyllis Palmer," Maureen said in an unnecessary whisper. "You know, the woman everyone calls Nurse Ratched.

That was the second time Loralin was in shock that day. How had she never known that her old nemesis and the chef had been married? She knew everything about everyone in Elk River, or so she'd thought. "Well, I'll be damned. I guess you learn something new every day."

*****

Devin came back from Lisa Marie's at around noon. The group from the hospital in Casper would be there in a couple of hours, and he'd promised to help set up. "Hey, so what is this party for?" he asked.

"It's for the people who got promoted when the new owners took over the hospital, and a meeting for the labor and delivery nurses." Loralin was out of sorts, and Devin couldn't figure out why.

"Is that a bad thing?" he asked. "I mean, doesn't Heather work there?"

"Yeah,' she said without any feeling. "But so does my old high school nemesis, and she still hates me and likes to make my life miserable."

"Oh, well, you can avoid her if you want. I'll stay and take care of things, and you can go home."

Loralin smiled at her best friend and accepted his smile in return. "It's not just that. Not only did she cause us to lose our chef for the day, but she is also going to make Heather's life a living hell."

"Oh well… wait a minute. How is she causing us to lose our chef for the day?"

Loralin explained about the chef and the nurse, then about how Miles picked her over the other woman. "So you see, she's already pissing me off, and she isn't even here yet."

"Me too," came a voice from behind them. They both recognized it.

"Heather, darling." Loralin greeted her with a kiss on the cheek. "What are you doing here so early?"

"The new boss bitch cut my shift."

*****

Devin left his Heather and Loralin to talk and went outside to see his father. "Hey, Dad!"

"Hey, boy, what's up?" Mark looked vital and alive for the first time in many years.

"Not much, Dad. We are getting ready for a big party in the dining room. Could you get three mixed flower bouquets from the flower garden and bring them into the lobby?"

"Sure thing, son."

Devin headed back into the inn and almost ran headlong into Miles. "Whoa, I'm sorry, man."

"It's okay," Miles said with a laugh. "I wasn't watching where I was going."

"What are you doing here?" Devin asked. "Did you see your daughter?"

Miles grabbed Devin's arm and steered him away from the inn. "I saw her. She's going to stay at my house after the party. Can I talk to you for a moment?"

"Uh, yeah sure," he said, following the detective. He knew it would be about his mother, and he dreaded the conversation. He didn't like to talk about it or think about it much.

"I just wanted to let you know that the doctors are concerned about your mother. She isn't eating properly and is getting dehydrated. They thought maybe a visit from you and your brother would help."

Devin knew what he wanted to say, but he worried that it would sound too harsh. He said it anyway. "She did this to herself. I don't think she'll want to see me right now. I won't be kind."

Miles looked at the young man whom he was becoming fond of. "You know, maybe she doesn't need or want kindness. Maybe she just needs to know that you are doing okay. That's what she did, didn't mess you up too badly."

Devin walked toward the river and heard Miles following him. "She did mess us up, though! My dad sold his family business and moved to a new country just to be close to her. How is that not messed up? And let's not even get into what's going on with Trevor. He's having nightmares every night."

"And what about you?" Miles asked. "What has this done to you?"

"It's made me angry!" he snarled. "She tried to kill the person I love most in this world. I hate her for that, but I also love her because she's my mother. Damn it, Miles, she ruined everything."

"Then go to her and tell her that. Take Trevor and let him tell her how he's feeling. Let her know how well your dad is doing now. She needs to know this, to know what's going on in your life. And you need to tell her just as much as she needs to hear it. You'll never heal if you don't."

"Yeah, maybe," he murmured. "I just don't know, Miles. I

don't know which way is up anymore." Devin took off for the river, and Miles headed back to his car. He'd done all he could.

As the shining, flowing river came into sight, Devin finally slowed down. He knew he should feel the heat of the noonday sun shining overhead, but he didn't. All he felt was cold, in his bones and on his skin. His mind was racing so fast that he thought he might explode. He needed to slow it down and think. He hoped the sights and sounds of the river would help.

Once he reached the bank, he stopped and stood with his eyes closed. The sound of the rushing water seemed to be sweeping away some of the confusion in his mind. "What do I do, Pop?" Oh, how he wished his grandfather were still alive. He could solve any problem. At least he had when he was a child. Maybe even this would be too much for him, though.

"Devin."

"Hi, Loralin. You can come closer." He realized he needed his best friend at his side; she and her inn were his future.

"Miles said you might need me." Her voice was soft and comforting.

"He was right. I don't know what to do, Loralin?" She could hear in his voice that he was crying.

"Hey, I'm right here," she murmured, walking up beside him. "Always."

He turned to Loralin and accepted her hug. "Thank you. I can't say it enough. You have completely changed my life, and I don't know what I'd do without you in it. Except, how did I suddenly become a hugger?"

"I told you you would, and I need you in my life too," she said, looking into his eyes. "I guess it's you and me against all the mysteries of the world."

"Always."

About the Author

JJ Weatherill is the author of 19 adult and young adult romance novels (JJ Ellis). She is a writer, graphic designer and long-distance mom to five kids. She enjoys reading, writing, graphic design, and watching cop shows on TV. She is having the time of her life writing cozy mysteries and can't wait to show you what's to come in the Robbin's Inn Mystery series. Grand Opening for Murder (book 1) and Promoted and Dead (book 2) are being published on the same day for the convenience of her readers. Book 3, A Death in Tassie, is coming soon! (Grand Opening for Murder was previously released under her original pen name of JJ Ellis but is no longer available for sale.)